OF HUMAN CARNAGE

ODESSA 1918–1920

" 'Odessa tells stories,' writes Avigdor Hameiri, and he has collected them in this book, a savage, surreal exploration of the cruelties of the Russian Civil War in Ukraine. Each story is a snapshot of the war of all against all, the descent into violence, that made the Great War of 1914–18 appear civilized in comparison."

Jay Winter
Yale University

"Avigdor Hameiri, a restlessly original pioneer of modern Hebrew literature, came to revolutionary Odessa after his ordeals as a Russian prisoner during the First World War. What he found there, however, was not a new dawn of hope but a nightmare of factional violence in which Red and White forces both reserved a special malice for the city's Jews. Shocking in its content, bracing in its form, *Of Human Carnage* is a 'movie novel' composed of brief scenes of horror, absurdity and occasional nobility.

Hameiri, who would go on to write two classic autobiographical novels of his wartime experience after he emigrated to 1920s Palestine, mixes snapshot realism with grotesque fables and a pitch-dark humour suited to the 'city of eternal jokes' that kept jesting even in the jaws of hell. His cinematic tales have a visceral impact and savage irony that sometimes recall the great Russian-language witness of Odessa in tumult, Isaac Babel. Peter Appelbaum's vivid and robust translation finds a compelling English voice for these dispatches from a time and place where terrifying chaos inspired stories filled with 'Jewish laughter… basted with tears'."

Boyd Tonkin
Former Literary Editor of *The Independent*
Author of *The 100 Best Novels in Translation*

OF HUMAN CARNAGE

ODESSA 1918–1920

Avigdor Hameiri

Translated and edited by
Peter C. Appelbaum

With an introduction by Dan Hecht

A joint publication between

BLACK
WIDOW
PRESS

The publication of this work was made possible by a generous grant from the Max and Anna Levinson Foundation and the assistance of Rachel Blackmon and Jim Kates, and Zephyr Press.

Black Widow Press is an imprint of Commonwealth Books, Inc., Boston, MA. Distributed to the trade by NBN (National Book Network) throughout North America, Canada, and the U.K. All Black Widow Press books are printed on acid-free paper, and glued into bindings. Black Widow Press and its logo are registered trademarks of Commonwealth Books, Inc.

Joseph S. Phillips and Susan J. Wood, Ph.D., Publishers
www.blackwidowpress.com

Stone Tower Press is a Rhode Island corporation. All design, production, and printing is done in the United States.

Publisher: Timothy J. Demy, Ph.D.
www.stonetowerpress.com

Cover Art: Abraham Manievich, *Destruction of the Ghetto, Kiev,* 1919, oil on canvas, The Jewish Museum (Gift of Deana Bezark).

Design, Typesetting & Production: Kerrie Kemperman

ISBN-13: 978-1-7338924-5-2

Printed in the United States
10 9 8 7 6 5 4 3 2 1

Contents

Introduction
"Odessa: Silent Film — Tragedy of a City in Avigdor Hameiri's Picture Novel"

Dan Hecht, Department of Literature, Tel Aviv University

The names of many central literary and Zionist personalities, such as Ahad Ha'am, Simon Dubnow, S. Y. Abramovich (Mendele Moher Sforim), Mosheh Leib Lilienblum, Yehudah Leib (Leon) Pinsker, Simon Frug, Yehoshua Rawnitzki, Elhanan Lewinsky, and of course the Hebrew national poet Hayim Nahman Bialik,[1] were associated with Odessa. The young poet Avigdor Feuerstein (later Hameiri) arrived at the Black Sea port from Kiev after Russia withdrew from the First World War and, as a Hungarian officer, he was released from captivity. "Amongst the yearnings, longings, hopes, and abject despair in my dreams of redemption during the hell of Siberian captivity, the longing for Odessa soared above all: Jerusalem of the Ukraine, center for Hebrew authors and Hebrew literature!"[2] Hameiri yearned to belong, for the first time in his life, to a circle of prominent Hebrew authors, to be in the center of it all. As an author in Budapest, he mainly moved amongst the circle of Hungarian Bohemians, yet was still able to publish some of his poems in the Odessa journal *HaShiloah.* According to the literary scholar Dan Meron, "Odessa was a kind of a honeycomb that spread its sweet attraction from afar to young Jews all over Russia who thirsted for knowledge."[3] If Russian Jewish youth expressed such feelings, how much stronger was the feeling of a Hungarian writer working far away from any center of Jewish culture.

But the city which Hameiri encountered had changed completely from the Odessa before war and revolution. It had ceased to be a center of Hebrew activity and ferment. The war had caused printing presses to idle, and manuscripts sat around unwanted and unread. The economic situation of writers and printers deteriorated more rapidly and severely, and the Civil War that broke out after the 1917 Bolshevik Revolution brought with it a violent wave of terrifying anti-Jewish pogroms. The Jews of Ukraine were used to anti-Jewish riots and oppressive decrees, but nothing could have prepared them for the extent of the horror which crashed over them at the end of the First World War, and the power of the Russian Civil War. "At an hour that calls out for love and unity, equality and freedom, an hour during which, before our very eyes, the visions of grand social prophecy seem to becoming realized, and all nations and men make peace covenants with one another—at this same hour the Jews of Ukraine are being subjected to a flood of tragedy and suffering, persecution and murder, whose like has not been seen before. Hundreds of cities and towns have been destroyed, all their possessions taken as booty, tens of thousands of people killed, thousands of maidens and women raped. It isn't in the power of man to relate everything that has happened."[4]

The condition in the city was unbearable, and a group of writers headed by Bialik and including Hameiri, took the step, as Zionists, of requesting permission to leave Russia together with their manuscripts. Their entreaties found a willing ear in Maxim Gorky,[5] who interceded on their behalf. Permission was eventually granted, thereby writing the final word on the history of Hebrew literature in Odessa. On board the *Anastasia* on its way to Istanbul, Hameiri wrote: "I have surely left you and will travel far away, homeward bound. Behold: the waves of the Black Sea rejoice with me."[6]

Immediately upon arrival in Israel in August 1921, Hameiri began to publish a series of stories in the newspaper *Haaretz*, entitled: "Odessa: Silent Film," consisting of short fragments of life from the bleeding city resembling movie scenes.[7] "I was witness to this upheaval in Odessa between 1919 and 1920, and photographed several moments of it. I filmed it — not as an enthusiastic tourist carrying binoculars. I wanted to refine and combine the sharp fragments into a round whole, as part of a movie novel..."[8] With rigid realism and awesome transparency, Hameiri succeeds in describing short moments of charged reality from his difficult experiences during the Civil War in Odessa after the October Revolution. These images purportedly represent objective reality, in which the Jews of the city have become trampled chiefly under the boot of Cossack cruelty, but are also subjected to great cruelty by both Red soldiers, and Denikin's White troops.[9] The first section published comprised four such "scenes," whose purpose was, as it were, to remove the ugly mask from the revolution that Hameiri had witnessed after the first violent attraction of the Great War, despite its initial lofty and idealistic slogans. "We saw yesterday's 'saints' that became today's villians; we saw proletarians, who became members of the bourgeoisie over-night." He wrote in his private forum *Lev Hadash*.[10]

In nearly each story, one may recognize Hameiri's knack for molding the story material, characters and setting, to constitute a clear and lucid personal statement concerning the described scene. Sometimes one statement is more complicated than another, sometimes one counteracts the one preceding it, but each story reflects a value that leaves almost no place for reservations. Hameiri transmits the information as crudely as possible, devoid of filters or superfluous additions. However, the materials from which these stories have been established are constructed in a manner that forms a meaning which is anything but objective. Some of the stories describing Bolshevik activities during the Civil War allow the reader a look into how Hameiri himself perceives the situation:

> Thieves, whores, jail refugees, yesterday's drunkards, amongst them yesterday's officers who have become world-saviors in one night.

> Gangs of such fellows spread into every city, into every house, "rich" and not so rich, in front of household members who stand with eyes red as demons — they dispose of household possessions as if they were theirs. [11]

In his later children's book *Animal Wisdom*, Hameiri satirically described the Russian Civil War as a fight between wild animals and cattle, suitably toned down for younger readers:

> Recently, the wild and domesticated animal within Man have tried to differentiate one from the other. The first are called "bourgeoisie," the second "proletarians." In Russia, the cattle have

risen up against the wild animals and devoured them, but no one could tell that they had done so.[12]

For Hameiri — who up to now had only published poetry books and columns in newspapers and periodicals — these were his first prose works to be published. They represent a kind of caesura, an intermediary between poetry and prose. The short flashes of prose are effective in transmitting the routine, banal violence in Odessa on the eve of the Civil War. The stories begin in chronological order when the army enters Odessa, imposing terror and chaos in the streets. The stories which follow were published over the next few years, and in 1929 the entire book, *Of Human Carnage* — the sixth book in Hameiri's collected works — was published. It included both the first, and all the later terrible experiences of Odessa's Jews until the last story which takes place in Istanbul, after Hameiri and his author friends have already left Odessa for Israel. In his introduction, as would become routine in all his books based upon personal experiences, Hameiri writes that this silent movie has no bias, for or against: "The movie camera has seen neither Lenin[13] nor Denikin, It just sees the wild animal that is man, and man, who is even worse than that." The literal name of the anthology, "From between the Man's Teeth," is derived from a poem by Yehuda Leib Gordon entitled: "From Between the Lion's Teeth," which depicts the cruel Roman colosseum in which men fought lions. After his harrowing experiences as a Russian prisoner of war, Hameiri sees cruel man as a beast of prey:[14]

By the hands of man, by the hands of man
Look into his face and do not shed tears,
Do not entreat him and do not groan
Lest he hear you.

Lest he see you dissolving alive
And calmly ask "Is this hard to bear?"
Afterwards — he smiles and lights up a cigar
And goes in for dinner.

By the hands of man, by the hands of man,
Who hates God and delivers his victim up to him,
While He sits in heaven and laughs
At man's fate.[15]

The first few stories in *Of Human Carnage* are very short
indeed and all take place in the streets of Odessa — artisans,
old people, children. All are reported as objective images:
mostly violent momentary scenes, impersonal and incidental:

Jews, young and old, are selling cigarettes on
the sidewalk. The city is like a boiling brew.
The regiment only conquered the city a few
hours ago — and they are selling cigarettes.

Shots of varying intensity can still be heard in
and outside the city — and they are selling
cigarettes.

The battalion that conquered the city has left
a line of terrifying pogroms in the wake of
its victorious advance — and they are selling
cigarettes.[16]

Hameiri pragmatically presents slivers of life in the difficult daily reality of time and place, with flickering lights like a
camera's lens shutter. In this way, the inner rhythm and dialec-
tic repetitiveness of the never-ending cycle of violence in
Odessa is revealed, with no settled routine, apathy, and hope-
lessness all at the same time. These momentary stories do not
represent Hameiri's usual prose, although their content echoes
in his other books. He tries to imitate by literary means the
natural sequence of a silent movie, in which each frame flashes
— a momentary image of one episode from the period's stormy
reality. These images sometimes reflect moments which are almost completely divorced from general relationships: people
without names or real involvement by the observer. Further-
more, the anthology *Of Human Carnage* also reveals the evo-
lution in Hameiri's literature, with quasi-documentary realism
changing into more designed stories, longer, more structured
and sometimes exaggerated in style with stronger and more
colorful character representation. Several later stories have early
features which would become clear foundations of Hameiri's
prose writings, expressed with great vigor in his war literature.

Some of the stories reveal the first signs of fantasy which
sometimes gave rise to criticism of Hameiri's prose due to lack
of credibility. Such stories are longer, and deviate from the
structured realism of his momentary reflections, flashes of reality that require only one image — although well "stage pro-

duced" — but credible from a stylistic point of view. Short scenes now give rise to narratives with a clear beginning, middle, and end. Amongst them is the story entitled "The Heretic."[17] The hero is a modern day 19th century enlightened hero ensnared in the magic of socialism, who returns to destroy his Hasidic village and then commits suicide. In "A Thousand," a white general has set himself the task of killing 1,000 Jews,[18] and "The *Almaz*" is about a legendary ship of suffering which has been turned into a tribunal, a sort of Red Guard field court martial.[19] All these are tales of horror which do not flinch from graphic descriptions of violence and terror, at times almost stylistically over the top because of their unnaturalness. In this way, they contrast with the first hyper-realistic stories in the anthology.

The ship *Almaz*, for example, describes a terrifying underwater monstrosity whose name alone strikes fear in one's heart. These stories also contain an element of craziness and insanity which grips the main protagonists. A man who has dived under the Black Sea near the ship's stern imagines that he sees men praying on the sea bed (to which they were sunk head first by large stones, feet up), and goes mad. The story "Him" presents the mysterious image of a monstrous, mythologic executioner who answers to the name "Him," obsessed about getting his hands on the Tsar. The quality of these stories resembles Hameiri's short war stories, which appeared contemporaneously in newspapers and periodicals. The latter contain fantastic prose from the front and are more identifiable with Hameiri's personal war experiences than with his documentary storytelling.

The uniqueness of *Of Human Carnage*, lies in the gradual transition, in one anthology, from realism to fantasy. This translation, which appears in English for the first time, provides an uncommon glimpse into the early work of a uniquely gifted Hebrew author about a dark, terrifying period in Jewish history in a city once the aspiration of young Jews looking to fulfil their dreams: a city identified with *Haskalah,* Zionism and literature which became in the words of Ezekiel a "reckless, miserable whore" before Hameiri's eyes. As stated above, these stories contain the first prose offspring of an extremely talented man who wrote in almost every possible form of the Hebrew language. They illuminate an additional aspect of his writings that has, until now, received little attention. The very short cinematic stories comprise a separate and distinct part of his writings. Combination of the latter with the more structured stories permit a broader look into Hameiri's development as a prose writer: a transition from cinematic hyperrealism to multilayered stories combining documentary description of people, places and real occurrences with fantasy and supernatural elements — features that would remain a hallmark of Hameiri's future writings.

Translator's Note

Of Human Carnage takes up where Avigdor Hameiri left off during the past few chapters of his second war novel, *Bagehinom Shel Mata (Hell on Earth)*. Indeed, a few of the episodes are summarized in the latter book. Hameiri finds himself in Odessa just in time to witness the brutal fight between Red and Whites of the Russian Civil War. His credentials as a former Austro-Hungarian prisoner of war make him acceptable to both Reds and Whites, neither of whom suspect him of counter-revolutionary activities, and he is granted extraordinary access to both sides. His access to the Cheka is described in the last chapter of *Hell on Earth*. There is no reason to suspect that these stories reflect — in principle — anything more or less than the truth. The fevered hallucinations of *Hell on Earth* have disappeared and the style is straight, uncomplicated, and (for Hameiri) transparent. At the end of the book Ginda Abramovna (whom Hameiri had met in Kiev while still a prisoner), reappears and travels with him to Israel. Bialik and Kleinman (who had secured Palestine entry permits) and a number of other notables accompany them. As far as could be ascertained, the actual events described in these short stories — terrible as they are — are accurate reflections of the chaotic times during the Russian Civil War. Of course, there are some fantasies mixed in.

This book is dedicated to the memory of my Hebrew mentor Siegbert Silbermann z'l. I thank the Shapira brothers for copyright approval to translate their grandfather's work, and Hillel Halkin, Avner Holtzman and Glenda Abramson for translation advice. As always, loving thanks to my wife and daughter for their support.

Peter C. Appelbaum
Land O Lakes, FL
January 2020

Dedication

To a bright and shining daughter of Odessa, Linta Asharshali,

from far away. With devotion and fateful humility

Avigdor

Author's Preface

A nightmarish silent movie. The film does not consist of huge amounts of celluloid. Just the opposite: it is quite short. Only a few small reels, through which two years pass: 1918–1920 in Odessa. Mother Odessa, protector and nurturer of Ukraine, Queen of the South, has turned, during the past 2 years, into a wanton, miserable whore, shrugging off her successive dearly beloved leaders like filthy undergarments, and presenting visitors with an artificially clean exterior, like a Potemkin village.

An unbiased movie, neither for nor against. The movie camera has seen neither Lenin nor Denikin. It just sees the wild animal that is man, and man, who is even worse than that.

Is there such a thing as revolution for its own sake? A revolution is nothing but an opportunity for a satanic masked ball in which the devil can work his will.

An engagement party between Lenin and Denikin. The Russian bear has become engaged to the widow, Odessa the Fair, and partied in chaotic abandon. A blood feast has been prepared, and during one dark night, we find ourselves in the jaws of death.

Kushta,[20] Tammuz 1921

Revolution[21]

The most sought after but at the same most terrible phenomenon on the face of the earth.

The sick soul of humanity lies on the operating table. A strange condition: A tiny part is hypertrophied, as if suffering from elephantiasis,[22] the rest is skin and bone.

This is not the first time that surgeons have practiced their art. They have even partially succeeded in straightening out the hideous hypertrophy.

This time, Professors Lenin and Trotsky[23] have decided to perform the final operation: to mercilessly extirpate the portion with elephantiasis from the rest of the body. Mercy plays no part in their operation. They use all their surgical equipment, starting with scalpels and ending with bandages.

But while they work it becomes clear that they are also operating on living subjects: limbs, blood vessels, muscles, white blood cells, parts of the brain: they pitilessly cut, remove and tear as they please. Mercy is not part of this surgery. Chaos reigns.

I was in Odessa from 1919 and 1920 during this earth-shaking tumult, and photographed several moments during it.

I photographed — but not as an amateur enthusiast with binoculars over my shoulder. I wanted to combine all photographs into a movie — a novel called *The Great Operation,* to help the patient from *The Great Madness*[24] recover, to give him voice, and end the film with a blessing: "Blessed be he who heals."

But meanwhile other doctors have arrived on the scene, feverishly cutting out body parts. They extirpate each other's existence like removing organs, with instruments that they have liberated for their own benefit.

In the meanwhile, I have become old.

I have learned that special abilities are needed for a revolution. It is not enough to appreciate and advocate it; one must also learn to bear its heavy burden, and be operated and experimented upon by it, physically and mentally, renouncing bodily and ethical integrity.

It appears that I don't have this talent.

The subject, placed upon the operating table, tries to solve the puzzle: how best to commit suicide.

I hope not to have to see this in the flesh,[25] because I have no talent for it either.

1.
Success

A bright, sunny day.

Pavement pedestrians, mainly Jews.

Cossacks, individually and in gangs, pass through the main street, one after the other. The last gang has already passed through. Pedestrians observe them leaving.

A single Cossack races past on his horse.

He suddenly stops, and points to one of the pedestrians. "Come here!"

The man hurries over with exaggerated rapidity. A Jew, dressed in winter clothing, with an expensive karakul Astrakhan hat on his head.

The Cossack bends over from his horse, snatches the expensive hat from the Jew's head, spurs his horse on, and flies off.

The Jew looks behind him, observes alertly — and then — he smiles.

He is happy that the Cossack didn't split his head open with nagaika or sabre.

2.

A Russian

Jews, young and old, are selling cigarettes on the sidewalk. The city is like a boiling military and civilian brew. The regiment only conquered the city a few hours ago — and they are selling cigarettes.

Shots of varying intensity can still be heard in and outside the city — and they are selling cigarettes.

The battalion that has conquered the city has left a line of mutilated corpses from terrifying pogroms in the wake of its victorious advance — and they are selling cigarettes.

A soldier passes by and wants to buy some cigarettes.

"How much for ten?"

"A hundred rubles. Best quality."

"A hundred rubles! You leprous Jewish bastard! Here are 10 rubles for you."

The Jew grimaces with a forced smile.

"Impossible."

The Jew and the Cossack bargain.

Berating, obscenities, curses. The Jew puts the cigarettes back into the box.

The soldier takes out his revolver and — shoots the Jew.

The Jew falls down dead.

The soldier takes out 10 rubles, puts them on the box, takes out ten cigarettes, and leaves.

3.
Custom

Yesterday victorious soldiers entered the city.

Riders, cannons, baggage wagons, and Cossacks compete for who can make the most noise. A large freight wagon full of armed soldiers rumbles by.

Suddenly a shot is heard, followed by another shot. One of the soldiers in the freight wagon has shot a Jew and his wife.

They both fall down dead in the street.

The other sidewalk pedestrians look at the dead Jews for one terrified tiny moment, then go on their way.

The freight train with the soldiers also goes on its way. After all, nothing unusual has happened.

4.
Peace

A Jew stands at his small sidewalk table, selling pastries.

One soldier comes up to him, followed by another.

They say something to him — and then take all the money in the chest of his small table. They simply take it, and walk off, without saying a word.

The Jew opens his mouth, wanting to implore them to return his money; but thinks better of it.

He makes a despairing gesture. May they all burn in hell.

He starts to collect up his meager possessions, and go home.

Suddenly, a cry:

"Jew! Jew! Jew!"

The Jew's face brightens. Are they poking fun at him, or do they want to return his money? I see them holding his money in their hands.

He stands for a moment, then takes a step towards them.

The soldiers come up and show him the money that they robbed from him.

"Leprous Jew bastard! These notes are forged!"

They demand replacement.

The Jew takes money from his pocket and exchanges the notes.

They part in peace.

5.
Dance for the Dead[26]

A clear day after a rainy night.

The usual street activity. People selling pretzels, speckled pastries, papirosas, combs, broken pots, rags, implement parts, empty bottles, rotten fruit and miscellaneous half-broken objects that, after years of repair, have eventually become trampled into a garbage heap by roosters' feet.

Amongst the crowd: two Jewish musicians.

That is to say: a blind man is playing, the other, a shrewd character, is singing.

Different kinds of songs and ditties: Jewish, Russian, Hebrew, Ukrainian — even German, as it were.

They stand on the sidewalk, behind a muddy puddle, making music.

No one takes any notice.

A village farmer arrives.

It seems as if he has just come from the village.

From his face we can see that he has had enough to eat; he is short-statured but solidly built.

His clothes are filthy, but without holes.

He walks somewhat hesitantly, stumbling slightly.

He is not completely sozzled yet, but is already quite tipsy.

He comes up to the musicians and looks at them.

He scratches his neck — thinking.

The Jew who is singing notices him and starts singing a Ukrainian ditty.

The farmer makes a casual movement, thrusts his hand into a deep pocket, takes out some banknotes, and gives them to the singer.

The singer bows in thanks, turns behind him to the musician who understands what he means, and adds zest to his playing.

They sing sweet songs more intensely,[27] trillingly, their lips entreating[28] with purity, tenderness, and outpouring of their souls to the Lord.

The farmer listens carefully, observes, and listens again.

He motions them to stop.

"Stop, stop. Not this."

The musicians bow their heads humbly.

"What do you want to hear?"

"Play this for me: Ha-Ha-T-Ra-Ta-Ta!"

The musicians understand, and start playing and singing his tune.

The farmer listens, enjoys the song, walks to and fro, and makes an impatient gesture:

"Quicker! Quicker: Tar-Ra-Ra! Ha-Ha-Tara!"

The musicians speed their pace up rapidly, nimbly, hastily, loudly, joyfully, forcefully.

The farmer accompanies them, first with his hands, then with his head, then his legs — and after a minute or so he is dancing, prancing reveling, frolicking. Ho-Ha! Ta-Ra-Ra! He jumps to and fro in the muddy puddle, water bubbles beneath his heavy boots, mud splashes on his clothes, body and mouth. Who cares?! Play — here is more money. Money isn't worth the paper it's printed on! Ho-Ha-Hoi! Music, life, happiness, rejoicing! He throws his hat to the devil. Play,

accursed Jews! Play! Play! Ho-R-Ra! O-A-Ta! He reaches
out to the singer: so, together! O-R-Ra! O-R-Ram-Tam-
Tam! Ho-Oy-Oy!

6.

Children

Two boys playing on the sidewalk.

They cross into the middle of the road.

A necklace of bloody drops can be seen along the length of the road. During the night the bodies of those condemned to death were taken to the cemetery by car. Blood has dripped out of the automobiles onto the road.

The boys stand on the bloody eruption, and observe.

"Blood" one says.

"Blood" the other boy agrees.

"Human blood!" says the first, with an air of expertise.

"No," says the second, "animal blood."

"You can't tell the difference between human and animal blood. I can."

"My father is a butcher. Animal blood doesn't look like this. This is human blood."

"My father," answers the second, "is a *shochet*.[29] This is bird blood, from a dove and a rooster."

"Lies. Your father is not a *shochet*. Complete lies! This is human blood!"

"You are also a liar. Your father is not a butcher! This is animal blood!"

"Even if that were true," says the first boy, "I still know that it is human blood, because it is the blood of my uncle, my mother's brother, Yaakov Isiewitz. They shot him yesterday. They locked him up, then shot him, and brought his body to the cemetery by car; this is his blood! Even if you burst, you can't change that!"

The second boy blushes with anger and confusion.

He thinks a bit, vacillates this way and that, and then says decisively:

"Me too," — he stammers, "Me too."

"What? What do you mean 'me too?' Are you trying to lie again?"

The second boy almost bursts with grief.

Suddenly he sees another bloody eruption on the road behind him: his faces blazes, he runs a few steps to it, and says proudly:

"This is my mother's blood!"

"I knew it! I knew that you would lie! Hasn't your mother died already? Didn't you say yesterday that your mother was murdered in the town — in the village of Zilivanka? You don't even have a mother — and this is human blood! You don't even have a mother!"

"Yes it is true — I don't have a mother. But, if I had one," — the second boy tries to extricate himself — "if I had a mother, she would have been killed in the town yesterday like your uncle was! You can be sure of that!"

The first boy bursts out laughing:

"Ha-Ha-Ha! They wouldn't have murdered her! Only men are murdered, not women! They killed my uncle two days ago, and this is his blood!"

"If that is true," the second attempts with his last strength — "be warned that tomorrow they will arrest my father! Yes, they will kill him! Just like your uncle! Be warned!"

"Rubbish! Your father is not a smart operator, like my uncle was! Everyone knew that my uncle was an operator, and they don't know your father at all! Aha! This is human blood, my uncle's blood!"

The second boy feels completely beaten. He thinks for a bit, stands erect, straightens his small coat and says:

"I'm going to tell everyone that my father is a smart operator as well! You'll see! I'm going to tell everyone!"

He walks off.

7.
Extremism

I'm walking in the road near an orphanage.

A sudden noise: I hear voices calling to me:

"Uncle! Hey, uncle! Is there a God, or not?"

I stand confused for a few moments: how should I reply?

One of them interprets my confusion, saying to his friend:

"You see? You see? He says there is no God!"

"That's a lie! He says that there *is* a God!"

"That's a lie," says the first child, turning to me again. "Is it really true that there is no God?"

I become curious to know the cause of this argument.

I nod my head, and say:

"There is a God!"

"Aha!" The second child skips victoriously. "Aha! — there is a God!"

When the first one sees that he is beaten, he says:

"He doesn't know with certainty — nobody does. There is no God. Our teacher knows better than he does!"

"The teacher knows," says the second, "and my father knows as well, better than the teacher, and my father says there *is* a God!"

"If that's the case," says the first, descending from the window angrily, "I'll go and tell the teacher! I'll go and tell her!"

He takes a few steps forward, looks behind him, and adds:

"I'll tell the teacher, and you won't get any dinner this evening!"

The second becomes a little scared, his face whitens — he looks backwards at his departing friend; when he has disappeared, he turns to a little girl near him, shrugs his shoulders, and says with equanimity:

"Let him go. Let him tell. I'm not scared. In any case tomorrow is Yom Kippur and this evening it is forbidden to eat dinner! Let him go and tell! Isn't it true, Devorah? There really is a God!"

8.
The Law

Forced labor recruitment has turned the city into a sweaty melting pot.

A long line of people waiting to be released stands in front of the Labor Commissariat.

The line is a quarter the length of the city, about 200 people. Each one stands — request in hand.

The "line" is seething. Each one is suspicious that the other has illegally stolen his place. Arguments, quarrels, cursing, pushing, shoving.

A line of many shades and parts.

Young, old, women, girls, students, workers, worn and tattered together with the elegant who haven't had time yet, as it were, to sell their decent clothes.

Heats scorches: foreheads sweat, hearts pound, hopes flicker: the commissariat hardly releases anyone. Very few win this lottery.

If only it would take just one day to render judgment!

But no: they stand here for four or five days and wait, and wait, and wait. They stand squashed, sweating, locking horns like angry bulls, quarreling, and waiting, until the work day ends and the "line" is postponed for yet another day. When will this end?

Meanwhile, the secret police come and arrest people in the line.

It is five days since the order came down for labor conscription, and they are still standing here with requests "to evade work!"

I stand in the line of wretched people, observing the faces of folk whose entire lives have been destroyed by this work decree.

In the midst of the line — I see a little three-wheeled carriage, inside a tiny pupil peeks out, from the eye of a one-handed amputee, with a head bigger than the rest of his maimed body combined.

I go up to him and ask:

"What are you doing here?"

No answer.

"Why are you here?"

No answer.

I raise my voice:

"What are you doing here, comrade?"

The amputee looks at me, opens his mouth, and asks:

"Ha?"

He is deaf.

I lean over his ear and ask his pardon.

He is not only deaf, but also dumb.

He stammers something, and smiles tragically.

"I don't understand!" I indicate to him.

Suddenly he takes his one hand out of his clothes and mumbles:

"Pencil."

I give him a pencil and piece of paper. He only has one hand.

His left hand is amputated. He writes something down with his right hand, and gives me his reply. I take the note and read:

"I was imprisoned all night for not having a 'work permit.'"

9.
A Ruse

Two of my acquaintances sit in a yard.

I lean out of my window which opens onto the yard, observing the two men below me. They are talking about this and that.

They speak about everything but the present.

They both look as if they have "come down in the world" — yesterday's bourgeoisie, today's beggars.

Suddenly they move nearer to each other.

They start speaking stealthily.

Fragments of words, whispers, hints: a unique language — the terrible language of the dejected, requiring experienced Soviet-Denikinist interpretation.

"Last night my house was searched. They emptied everything out as thoroughly as leaven before Pesach[30] and hardly left me with a pot to piss in."

Silence.

The second man:

"If only I knew that this would be the last search."

"Last? When will it be the last? When the Messiah comes. Apart from that, what do I care if it's the first or last search? It makes no difference — what else can they take? The pot on the wall?"

"What's under the pot?" the second man asks slyly.

"What? Under the pot? Are you making fun of me? I told you, they left me with nothing. They even took the silver gold-encrusted Magen David off my little girl's neck. They took — everything."

The second man lights a cigarette and sucks the smoke in greedily.

"I didn't know that you were such a no-hoper," he says through the smoke.

"And so?"

"What?"

"Don't despair"

"There is nothing one can do against such cunning thieves."

"If there is a thief, show yourself to be sneaky."[31]

The first man whispers into the second's ear:

"Talk of the devil, and he is sure to appear. You are still not safe. Your precious stone (diamond) is still in danger."

The second shows him a sign: "Not that."

"How?"

"It's in safe hands."

"Even if you put your nest amongst the stars — "[32]

The second leans over the first and whispers in his ear:

"Liza has it."

"Which Liza?"

"My sister, Liza Lazarovna."

"How? Your sister Liza Lazarovna? What are you chattering about? Didn't you bury her yesterday?"

"Yes, yes, she has it. My wife hid the stone in her hands, and so — "

Silence. The other man's eyes open wide: He lights up a cigarette, and slowly smokes it. He nods his head without looking his friend in the face, and says despairingly, with sad remorse:

"Who would think of such a thing?"

He breathes the cigarette in deeply, and repeats sorrowfully:

"Who would think of such a thing?"

10.
A Jew

The streets are in ferment.

They are searching Bialik's publishing house.

The printing paper is being confiscated.

The publishing house is wide open. Bialik stands in the middle of the room, trying to speak to the severe-looking government emissaries, who are doing what they regard as their duty.

His words are of no help at all.

There is confusion in the printing house.

The appropriators search, turn over, command, arrange, note down, vandalize.

One man is leading this mad orchestra.

He is a Jewish commissar.

There are four simple soldiers, but it is the one Jewish commissar who is doing all the damage.

He rapidly notes down all the paper in the printing press with zeal, energy and a unique type of enjoyment.

Suddenly he sees a pile of high-quality paper: he looks, and sees that something is already printed on it.

They are poems by Solomon ibn Gabirol.[33]

The commissar looks at the printed sheets, turns to the ordinary soldiers standing meekly and silently in their places, and says to them:

"Look comrades, how they have befouled this paper! What a pity!"

11.
A Proletarian

There is an anniversary celebration in the sanatorium. It's a whole year since the bourgeois hospital has been turned into property of the proletariat.

Speeches, orchestra, a people's play, songs, praises. And after all this — a banquet.

On the table — God knows where they all suddenly came from — champagne, ordinary wine, different dishes, and speeches. —

Around the table sit doctors, nurses, some soldiers, and commissars, all dressed in festive garb.

One guest stands out, dressed in simple workers' clothes. He sits amongst the other guests, and drinks, and drinks and drinks.

The physician-in-chief stands up and speaks: be has a sharp and gratingly melodious voice,[34] which become ever louder, noisier, striking the audience like lightning bolts:[35] "Yes, comrades, this is a new world, a sacred revolution, the blood-sucking leeches have been removed from the body politic, they have passed away like smoke. Everything, everything, is from, by and for the workers! Hurrah! Hurrah!"

After him the worker rises hesitantly, and mouths off the physician-in-chief's clichés. "Yes comrades: everything, is from, by and for the workers. Hurrah!"

He drops down into his chair.

Drinking, glasses clinking, the burst of uncorked bottles, music, noise — Hurrah!

Suddenly a sick man, dressed in hospital garb, approaches the table. He stands out like a sore thumb amongst the other guests dressed in their finest plumage. His face is white as a sheet, eyes sunken and bloodshot. He strikes the table edge with the clenched fist of his emaciated hand, causing some glasses to fall with a crash. He sways to and fro weakly, and cries in a hoarse, groaning voice:

"Lies! All lies! Not for — !"

He starts to cough and his face becomes greenish-red. His cough is horrible: productive, bubbling, hoarse, asphyxiating. After the coughing attack, he wants to say something else:

"You — drink — kha — kha — kha — you — you —"

He coughs, spits a gob of black blood onto the table, and moans:

"Drink this!"

He falls flat on his face to the ground, moaning with a hoarse sigh:

"This is for you — drink it — drink my blood! My blood!"

12.
Happiness

Towards evening.

Three children on the side of the main street.

They are rummaging for something in a garbage pile.

The children are torn and tattered, thin and pale. They rummage and rummage — and finally find something.

The rummaging becomes a competition: first one wins.

In the meanwhile, a little dog joins the small throng.

No problem: the dog joins in the rummaging. They find something.

They eat some of the things they find at once, others are put in a bowl. Lord knows what they collect there: potato and other peelings, cigarette pieces, bits of paper for heating, wood shavings, toothpicks. Everything is worth collecting.

Suddenly, a large dog arrives on the scene, growls at them fiercely, and chases them and the small dog away.

The terrified children recoil.

They look at the dog enviously.

The dog starts rummaging in the garbage.

"Come—" one child says to his friend despairingly, "let's go. This is Jasha's dog — I know him. He won't let us get near, and will take everything."

Not far behind them, a stunted boy child walks up to the large dog, sack in hand, and puts everything that the dog has scrabbled out for him into the sack.

Jasha is happy.

13.
Citizens

Two boys are sitting side by side on a garden bench overlooking the main street. Each one is busy cracking sunflower seeds. They say nothing to each other, just crack and spit out, crack and spit out. One boy is dark-haired, with large eyes and a high forehead. The other is pale and flaxen-blond. Both are dressed decently. They must be from "well-to-do" families, because they seem well-fed: apparently they haven't been stripped bare yet.

This goes on for quite a long time: no words are spoken.

Suddenly a car passes behind them.

The noise makes both boys turn their heads around, in the act of spitting out shells.

They spit shells in each others' faces.

Both redden with anger.

"You pig!" They say simultaneously.

The blond boy rises, and hits the second boy in the face with his balled fist.

The second kicks the first in the belly.

The rest follows spontaneously: blows, kicks, hats snatched off, faces scratched.

I rise and separate them.

Each one takes his hat off the ground and dusts it off. The dialogue goes as follows:

The blond one, with inner contempt, but quietly:

"Miserable Chekist!" (Chekist: member of the dreaded State "Emergency Commission" with life and death power).[36]

The second with the same contempt, but this time loudly:

"Hooligan! Child murderer!"

"Who can murder better than a Chekist?"

"Defiler of women!"

At the same time:

"Chekist! Chekist!"

The second draws himself to his full height and says, eyes blazing:

"So what if I am a Chekist! My father is one as well. and so are my mother (an obvious lie), brother and sister! Chekists are necessary to dispose of garbage like yourself!"

The second, as if standing up to expected danger:

"I could also become a Chekist if I wished! My uncle is a Chekist! He comes from Saratov!"

"The Chekists have already put your uncle from Saratov up against the wall and shot him!"

The blond boy becomes pale with anger:

"Last year alone, my father cut off forty Jewish mens' heads, and raped ten women!"

"Pogromchik!"

"Zhid!"[37]

The dark-haired boy scrutinizes the blond boy from top to toe. He wants to strike him but restrains himself. The blond boy balls his small fist, as if preparing for further battle:

"Yes, fithy Zhid! My father will kill you as well!"

Upon hearing this, the dark-haired boy, as if knowing exactly what to do, turns to leave. He walks a few steps, then turns back, and says decisively:

"He'll never be able to do it! I know you! I know where you all live!"

He walks away with confident step, and an air of vengeful disgust.

14.
A Proletarian Woman

Fear of the "Emergency Commission" casts an asphyxiating fog over the city.

More lists of official executions, more acquaintances killed, another list of Jewish prisoners.

It makes no difference: The *Tzeirei Zion*[38] meet and work in secret, read aloud news from their far-away homeland, which casts its glow on us from uncountable past generations and vast distances.

More strict searches, more terrible rumors.

It makes no difference. The hungry young men and women know no rest. But more than hunger for bread, they hunger and thirst for a new Hebrew word.

They come to us, we wretched gang of writers, with requests, demands, unending pleas.

"When will there be another 'anthology reading'?"

"When will you read something?"

"Please, let it be this coming Sabbath. Oh, please!"

We arrange an oral gathering, in the *yeshivah*[39] house.

This house is our "Nitzah's attic,"[40] where we take shelter from threats and violence.

Not with swords, spears or rifles.

But with Hebrew letters.

The hall is full to overflowing.

Each read or spoken word is swallowed with pure, child-like, sacred zeal.

Suddenly, the reader is interrupted in mid-sentence: an armed man appears at the door.

"Sh! — Sh! — " is heard from all sides.

The same is heard from near the door.

"Sh! — Sh" — says the armed angel of death. — "Sh! — Sh! Stay right where you are and don't move! You're all under arrest! Sit down quietly!"

The blood of the entire assembly freezes.

We all sit and wait in awe and dread

The "uniformed" man comes up to the table, revolver in hand.

I rise and give him the hand-written sheet from which I have been reading.

"Please. — "

He takes it with shining eyes and says:

"This is respectable material."

"You err, comrade. It is belletristic literature, no more than that."

"Yes, Yes. I know that."

He look at my hand-writing, and says:

"Hebrew?"

"Yes."

He says to me with victorious disparagement: — "Nu, did all these people come here just to hear belletristic Hebrew literature?"

The last few words are soaked with ridicule.

He changes the subject:

"Does everyone here understand Hebrew?"

"Certainly."

He smiles mockingly:

"Yes: we certainly know the 'belletristic literature' of Zionism."

"Please, comrade, there is no Zionism here. We are Hebrew writers only for the sake of Hebrew writing, with all the responsibilities that this entails."

"Where are you from?"

"Hungary."

"Aha. From Hungary. And when did you arrive here to make propaganda in our country?"

"I arrived here in 1916 as a prisoner of war, courtesy of your 'Brusilov Offensive.'"[41]

He looks at me and understands what I am trying to say.

"Nu — enough."

He turns to the men who have accompanied him, and says to us:

"Outside! Keep order! Don't try to escape: anyone who dares leave without permission will have himself to blame! He'll be shot on the spot!" —

We stand outside in line, in groups of four.

There are about 180 of us.

Two men stand at the gate and catch those who were late for the "assembly."

"Please," — they say to the latecomers mockingly, "please be so kind as to stand there in line."

At first the people are terrified, but, after a moment, they stand up for themselves:

"Ah — please."

The latecomers join our "throng," faces shining.

A young maiden comes to the gate, torn and threadbare, barefoot; no, worse than that — her shoes are so broken that it makes one weep with pity.

The "comrades" at the gate are not moved by the "proletarian" appearance of the girl, and bar her from entering.

"Entry into the yard is forbidden."

"Why? Must I be searched?" the girl asks, continuing without waiting for a reply:

"This yard is of no interest to me. I am on my way to the Hebrew 'anthology reading'" she says innocently.

"Ah! So you as well?" — The "comrades" scrutinize her from top to toe. "Go and join their 'line!'"

The young maiden understands the situation immediately: her face lights up joyfully.

"Please," she almost croons with happiness, "Certainly, comrades! With great pleasure! Thank you!"

She hurries to us and joins our throng.

15.
Solitary Confinement

After a few moments of silence, the entire road is in ferment.

"They have arrested the Zionists!" — the whisper goes around the large crowd. They stand on the sidewalk looking at us.

With trembling, pity and fear.

We walk away.

Into the arms of the Cheka.

Into the boiling courtyard of death, reeking of terror.

A long line: young man and women, white-haired old men, and children.

Around us a noise cuts cruelly through the air. The crying of Cossacks on horseback, surrounding us like an iron chain, brandishing their revolvers, yelling to the people in the street:

"Move! Onto the sidewalk! Nobody go near them!"

Then to us:

"Don't dare move out of the line! If you do, you'll be shot dead on the spot!"

The crowd in the street recoils. Shots echo in the air, followed by — silence. We walk on. —

Suddenly, amongst the sound of many treading feet and horses' hooves — the sound of a song.

At first only one, then two, then everyone joins in, including young women. The song gradually becomes a secret chorus: serious, deeply felt, an outpouring of the soul:

"As long as the Jewish spirit is yearning, Deep in the heart."[42] —

16.
Company

On the side of a boulevard.

Couples sit on benches, children on the ground.

Next to me: a young husband and wife.

Not far from us a little boy and girl play in the dust.

Suddenly they begin to quarrel:

"Barefoot twit!" the girl says.

"And you — you — you were a foundling!"

"You too! You too!"

"Not me!" — the boy says confidently. "I have a father, a mother, and everything! And you: you have nothing: no father, no mother!"

The young couple start to pay attention to the quarrel.

"Listen! Listen!" the young woman draws her husband's attention to what is going on.

The childrens' quarrel continues:

"You don't have anything either!" — the little girl says, face twisted with anguished anger.

"It's a lie! I do too have parents! If I want, I can hit you, kill you! If I wish, I can put you against the wall!"

He balls his small fist at the girl, raises his hand, and repeats:

"You don't have parents! I'll kill you!"

"Go!" The little girl's face is distorted with weeping. "Go away!"

"You're just a foundling!" the boy says again contemptuously, getting his hand ready: "You have nothing at all!"

"Not true!" the girl tries to fight back — "You're telling lies! I have a father, a mother, everything. I have many mothers and fathers in 'Sozibes'[43] (socialist-economic child care institute). I have many parents there, and everywhere else!" — She bursts into tears, raises her eyes, and sees the young couple on the bench; as if escaping from the devil, she hurries to the young woman, buries herself in her lap, and with her second hand, strokes the man's knee. She weeps bitterly:

"He says that I'm a foundling, without mother and father! Is that true or not? It isn't true! Isn't it true, that you are my mother and father?"

The young woman hugs the child, clasps her to her heart, and says with a voice choking with tears:

"Yes, my little dove, my little flower, you're my dear little daughter!"

She bursts into tears.

17.

Culture[44]

  The city has been resurrected from the dead. The trolley car is running.

Joy and gladness — the trolley car is running again.

Drunken White officers terrorize the city, beating passers-by with dog-whips. No matter — the trolley car is running.

Every day, every hour, bound Jews and other workers are led to the undiscovered country from whose bourn no traveller returns. No matter — at least the trolley car is running.

The new government has declared previous government's banknotes invalid, and the city is an empty vessel. No matter — the trolley car is running.

The road is full of starving beggars sprawling on the sidewalk, grabbing legs of passers-by, weeping bitterly and imploring them for a piece of bread — they all mean nothing.[45] The trolley car is running.

The trolley is full to overflowing.

People are squeezed into it like herrings in a barrel.

In one corner, a gang of Russian students who, this very night, affixed the seven seals of the intelligentsia onto their clothes, speak loudly and self-confidently, laugh in the faces of, and hurl high-minded phrases at, their fellow-passengers abusively.

Joy and gladness reigns.

The trolley-car stops.

A large crowd of people want to push in-between the already overcrowded passengers — but there is no room.

Suddenly, the students cry:

"Let the lady get on! Let her get on! Make room for a lady! There is surely place for one more lady."

This makes a good impression: they are well-mannered, courteous students after all! We haven't heard such courtesies for a long time!

The woman gets on with great difficulty.

The student's mocking abuse stops for a moment.

This too makes a good impression. They would not dare do this near a woman (would they?). Soon I understand what is going on: several of them are trying their best not to burst out laughing. They wink at each other, and laugh silently.

The people don't take notice of them: after all, they are young: what is more natural than for them to poke fun at people?

They carry on laughing silently.

Looking in the direction of the woman.

She feels that there is something wrong, moves angrily and blushes.

Suddenly the students burst out laughing. They can't contain themselves anymore.

The woman pushes her way towards the door, and waits impatiently for the trolley car to stop.

The trolley car stops and the woman gets out.

She only has to walk a few steps before a display opens up for all to see. A large hole has been cut by a scissors, in the back of the woman's black dress, showing her white petticoat underneath.

She walks along the length of the road, and doesn't know a thing.

The crowd in the road behind her roar with laughter.

A Jewish woman runs after her and alerts her as to what is happening.

The woman looks behind her, moans silently, begins to move as if drunkenly in the direction of the wall — faints, and falls helplessly to the ground.

18.
Luck

Thirty men have been "exchanged" from this world to the next.

The city is still in a ferment, air filled with the noise of cannon and rifle fire.

Bullets and pieces of exploding shrapnel whistle intermittently over the heads of passers-by. People flee from road to road, from corner to corner. Soldiers' shouts are mixed with the moans and death rattles of the wounded.

There is a "line" in one of the alleyways.

The line is quite long.

About 200 people stand in a long line in front of the bakery, pressed to the wall, waiting amidst the tumult for the chance to obtain a crust of bread.

Within the line: trembling, confusion. A grenade explodes in the air, and breaths are held for a few moments: arguments, curses.

"Please don't stick your head out!"

"I've had this place for a long time!"

"I've been standing here since dawn!"

"And I from yesterday evening!"

"That one over there — yes, the tall one! How did he get here?!"

"Put your hand over your mouth!"

"Filthy Jew bastard!"

"Fonye the thief!" (derogatory Russian nickname).[46]

And so on.

All because of a miserable place in line.

First come first served. Not only that, but for the one behind — let the devil take the hindmost.

The firing doesn't stop.

Neither does the cursing.

Suddenly — something in the air freezes everyone's blood.

A terrible silence.

A grenade. —

Faces grimace with terror, heads hunched between shoulders, breath held.

The huge explosion is deafening!

Cries, moans, people falling down. —

The grenade has exploded right in the line of people waiting for bread. Four people are killed instantly, one is badly wounded.

Everyone looks, eyes popping out of their heads at the torn, mutilated corpses lying in pools of blood.

They look — but do not budge from their place in line.

Frozen silence —

Soldiers come to carry the bodies away.

There is silent rejoicing, almost happiness, in the line.

Five places have opened up!

People lucky enough to take the emptied spots, stand with joyful, shining faces, heaving happy sighs of relief.

19.
Lunatic

Today there are frequent city-wide searches.

From all directions, armed gangs lead "criminals" to their terrible "judgment."

The criminal is surrounded by a narrow ring of soldiers with rifles and fixed bayonets.

Cries from every side:

"Move to the side or I shoot! Move to the side, I say!"

On the sidewalk, passers-by stop for a minute, looking at their wretched, arrested acquaintances — who have already given up on this world. Armed "officials," revolvers on their hips, look around the crowd searchingly, alert for the slightest utterance.

A single word against the government, or even the mouthing of a word to the prisoners — is enough for a "request" to join their throng.

In the midst of all this confusion — singing is heard.

A young Jewish man dressed in rags stands at the side of the road, face tuned to passers-by. Without even so much as a passing glance at the prisoners in the street, he stands and sings.

He doesn't sing for money, he sings for the sake of singing and for his own and others' enjoyment. He sings in Hebrew.

Cantorial chants.

He is the "city lunatic"; everyone knows him. He goes from courtyard to courtyard singing: a typical cantor's voice.

His voice is pleasant to the ear.

He sings the High Holiday melodies, with taste, earnestness, inner feeling, and sad cantorial embellishments, up and down the scale, with all his heart and soul.

"Slaves rule over us,[47] sla-v-es rule, oy, oy, oy, ru-l-e over us — us — rule over us — oy, tate,[48] rule —

R-u-l-e!"

When an "official" passes by him, he, takes a step or two in his direction, and trills in his face with special emphasis and heart-breaking grief:

"Slaves — oy, tate — s-l-a-v-e-s!"

20.
Prayer

The "lunatic" is the only man in the city who doesn't recognize the sovereignty of any Russian "dynasty." Why should he? They change almost every morning.

He is in his own world, standing and singing.

His tender, touching voice draws people to him.

After the wretched city has been occupied by the second government, there are yet more searches. (Everyone is on the prowl in this hopeless, abandoned country: everyone is looking for something). Once more, gangs of soldiers leading "criminals" to their deaths: we already know the picture all too well.

The lunatic sings:

He goes up and down the scale, with cantorial embellishments, with innermost grief and entreaty that penetrates the very heart and soul:

When one of the White officers passes by him, he walks towards him, and wails right in his ear:

"Pour out your wrath among the nations![49] Oy, tate zisse![50] Pour! P-o-u-r out your wrath! Among the nations! The n-a-t-i-o-n-s!"

21.
Generosity

A Jewish woman is selling pastries, cigarettes, candy, drinks, and various toys, necklaces, gold crucifixes (at least so it seems) and simple ornaments.

Passers-by stop for a minute, look, inspect — and walk on.

What is pleasing to the eye is the only enjoyment that those who own the world have not yet been able to destroy or damage.

The woman sits and dozes.

No one disturbs her.

Suddenly — a group of soldiers arrives.

Noise, drunken laughter, obscene Russian curses.

The highest ranking soldier stands alongside the "store."

"Sirs!" (now they are known as "sirs," not "comrades").

"Sirs! Stop and let's drink something!"

They stand around the woman's table and start to examine her merchandise.

"She has everything a man could desire!"

They start to select their drinks.

The woman hurries willingly to give them what they want.

The head of the group chooses what he wants, eats and drinks, and shares with his comrades:

"Eat, Sirs! Drink! Eat! Eat!" — (obscenity).

"Drink!" — (another obscenity).

The women selects, gives, makes suggestions.

"Sirs, try this one! It's very sweet — I baked it myself."

"Have you any vodka?"

The woman looks round her with fear and suspicion.

"Don't be afraid! Don't be afraid! Give it to us! We aren't Bolsheviks or Orthodox priests! Give us some!"

"I have some, but I don't know whether you'll like it. It's home-brewed, and very strong!"

"Give it to us!" — (an even worse obscenity).

The woman takes out a bottle, and the men drink.

One of the men says:

"This is not vodka, it's ____!" (please excuse me, but I can't write his exact words down). "But it's good: bitter and strong."

A second remarks:

"One can't even get drunk from this!"

A third:

"Never mind, it's drinkable! Strong and bitter!"

They eat and drink, drink and eat.

In the meanwhile, their mood turns happy and celebratory: mouths full, liquored up, curses and obscenities grate on the ear.

A crowd gathers in the street around the woman's stall. Passers-by stand, look, enjoy the spectacle, and the comrades — do as they wish.

Suddenly the senior officer turns to the crowd drink in hand:

"Drink up, Sirs! Drink with us! Ha! Drink!" (obscenity).

One of the bystanders, dressed in a torn army uniform, comes over, and takes a drink.

"Take this as well!"

He gives him pastries.

The man takes a drink, thanks him, and eats with appetite and shining eyes.

The senior officer turns to the rest of the crowd, giving them pretzels and drinks. They eat and drink. In the meanwhile, the officer's mood becomes more expansive: he draws near those who are about to go, doesn't allow them to leave the celebration[51] and makes them eat and drink. Suddenly he sees the toys and decorations:

"Give me some of these as well!"

The woman gives everything willingly and with alacrity, with joy and happiness.

He takes the necklaces, hangs them around his neck, puts rings on his fingers, and gives some to his comrades and the strangers standing around him.

"Hey, Sirs! Look at the beautiful things! Adorn yourselves! Beautify yourselves! Russia is rich! Take, ladies and gentlemen — take! Russia is rich! It has everything! Eat, drink, beautify yourselves, take! Ha!" (an unmentionable obscenity that applies to the entire world).

The small crowd takes, eats, drinks and adorns themselves, and gradually leave.

"Thank you! Thank you very much, sir! — thank you!"

The little store's merchandise has been almost completely exhausted.

The bowls of pastries are empty. The bottles are empty. Everyone smokes a cigarette: they put the others in their pockets.

And go on their way. —

The poor woman becomes pale. Her wide eyes fill with tears.

"Sirs, Sirs! Please pay! I am a poor widow-woman! — Please!" —

No one takes the slightest notice of her.
She wails, crying bitterly.
She takes the little that is left, and totters erratically
home with faltering steps: weeping, weeping. —

22.

Compassion

Days of "peaceful demonstration." Such a simple term.

The most charming innovation of the Russian Revolution.

It's real meaning: the authorities allow every worker to enter any house of the bourgeoisie, wherever and whenever he wants, and take everything he likes, for himself — Anything and everything is fair game.

Because the ordinary worker doesn't do this (not God forbid because he doesn't want to transgress the Tenth Commandment "Thou shalt not covet," but because he is afraid of the frequent "changes" of government hanging over each city), the authority does what it likes — in the persons of the "dregs of society."[52]

Thieves, prostitutes, prison escapees, yesterday's drunkards, amongst them yesterday's officers, who have achieved "fame and glory" overnight.

These gangs spread all over the city, burst into houses of the "rich," ordinary and poor, — right in front of their owners who stand there with hate-filled eyes, powerless to do anything about it — and do whatever they like.

I describe one such day to you:

"A peaceful day of demonstration," that slices the nerves in two and fills the eyes with blood.

No one dares say a word or lift a finger.

(One Jew dares — even if it's the last time in his life he dares to do something — he pulverizes the face of a "peaceful demonstrator," and afterwards commits suicide).

There are four "peaceful demonstrators" in the house that we are describing: three males — one commissar and two murderous thugs.

And a whore.

Please excuse me — this is not mere conjecture, or a derogatory name by the author — that is really her line of work.

She hasn't even thought it necessary to clean up the blue eye shadow and red paint on her face and lips for this mission.

They enter the apartment and begin to plunder it.

One man stands at the door, a second takes everything he likes in the house and places it in one pile.

The whore — adapts right away to the situation.

She finds a nice bonnet — and stuffs it into her bosom.

She finds a gold necklace, and puts it on.

She finds earrings: Not a minute to lose! She puts them on.

She finds a fan — into the bosom with it!

The woman of the house stands, pale as a sheet, as if already dead and abandoned.

Not one word escapes her lips.

She stands, her legs become weak and her knees knock.[53]

Suddenly the "silent demonstration" whore sees a gold ring with a precious stone on the hand of a young maiden standing next to the woman of the house.

This young girl is not part of the household. She has just arrived by chance, and now they don't allow her to leave.

She hasn't had a chance to hide her ring.

The female "government representative" looks at her expensive ring.

She lifts the pale finger and inspects it.

The woman of the house, who has stood frozen up till now, cannot take it anymore.

She says to the whore with a hoarse voice, dripping with blood:

"Please, comrade, you don't have permission to do this! She is not part of our family! She's a guest, who has just arrived!"

The comrades are furious at this chutzpah.[54]

The young girl appears to faint. Or does she?

No: She falls down on the sofa, dead from a fatal heart attack.

A small commotion — the man of the house pushes the "guard" at the doorstep aside, and runs to call a doctor, followed by his wife, shrieking wildly.

"A doctor! We need a doctor here!" —

The four comrades are left alone in the house.

They walk to and fro, and start grabbing things, hiding them in pockets, boots, bosom—any possible hiding place on their persons.

We stand at the window in the yard looking on, and understand nothing — why go to all this trouble?

Who prevents them from simply taking everything and leaving?

One of us whispers: "stolen water — "[55]

The maiden lies motionless — she is dead.

The "official whore" comes up to us and chases us from the window: "Go to hell!"

We leave the window in confusion; when we return after a minute, she is prising the ring off the dead girl's finger.

23.
The Artist

Fourier[56] said: "Every type of work gives birth to its own master."

The act of searching has become very important in Russia.

It is important for all types of government.

Why is this true? Because, every dynastic change and exchange begins and ends with searches.

The act of searching has turned into a true art form.

"The Jews and the bourgeoisie are experts in concealing the people's wealth." (According to one set of rulers the bourgeoisie are the culprits, the other blames the Jews). In either case, thorough, searches are the order of the day.

Every possible location or building has been used as a place of concealment.

For this reason there is no conceivable location or building that hasn't been penetrated by the searchers.

One way or the other, every Jewish Chaim-Shmerel has already been searched a thousand times.

Either as a Jew or as a member of the bourgeoisie.

Or as a Jewish-bourgeois.

Homes looks as if every leprous fungal contaminant mentioned in the Tractate *Nega'im*[57] has eaten them away.

Walls are peeling and broken; floors cracked and full of holes; ceilings perforated, torn and ripped; plates cracked; everything is left wide open to the elements.

Now — yet another search.

The owner of the house isn't afraid anymore.

Because there is nothing more to fear.

On the contrary: the searchers enter, the owner shakes the hand of one of them with a sense of calm satisfaction:

"Welcome. Please sit down!"

He gives him a chair, repeats his friendly welcome, shakes hands, and sits.

"Thank you very much" — the thief says, and plops into the chair, merrily drunk.

He finds a pack of cigarettes in his pocket and offers one to the owner.

After a few moments — the search begins.

As prescribed: methodically, seriously, diligently, thoroughly.

A friend of the owner is conductor of this little band: he understands, he is an expert — a true search artist.

When they find a suspicious place and his friends pounce on it — he sets their minds at rest.

"No, comrades, there is nothing here, so it would be stupid and useless to search. I know places like this."

When they finish their work — they depart.

Shaking hands politely with the owner.

"Goodbye!"

"Goodbye and good luck."

They part in peace.

I ask the owner, astonished:

"What's going on? Have you known this man for long?"

"Certainly! He is the master thief of Alexandrowka province![58] Petya the thief! He is the master thief of all governments, and my personal favorite under the present regime. He's a drunkard. However, the second regime doesn't give him anything to drink; then he attacks me and becomes quite belligerent. But Petya the thief is a likeable lad."

24.
Disguises

I meet two commissars whom I have known for a while.

The first is a simple Russian soldier, a barber in private life — he was my prisoner of war camp guard.

A quiet, good Russian lad, humble and tender-hearted.

The second is a young Lithuanian Jew, also known to me from my prisoner of war days — a *yeshivah bokher*[59] in private life.

A very nice lad, with a soft and gentle nature, filled with compassion, ready to give his friend the "shirt off his back."

But now they are commissars.

Both in uniform, walking rapidly and in great haste. Where?

"To the bourgeois, to fleece them a little. We need clothes! Come with us. It will be fun!"

I go and see what is happening.

First they go into a house full of worn out "soldiers" without uniforms, dressed in simple clothes.

They call about five out.

We walk off together.

On the way one of the commissars tells me:

"These are the men whom we have to clothe."

"With bourgeois clothes?" I ask.

"Yes."

"But how? Those people have civilian clothes, not uniforms."

They laugh:

"So what? Let them dress for once in expensive clothes! Ha Ha!"

Well, let's see what happens.

We enter a rich man's house.

After about 15 minutes, the occupants of the house have collected everything they own in one large pile.

"Take your clothes off as well!" one of the men commands.

The owner of the house implores:

"Are you going to leave us naked for the world to see?"

"No. Why naked? Take off your clothes, and we'll give you others."

No amount of imploring is of any use.

The occupants of the household — four males — take off all their clothes and hand them over.

The soldiers put the good clothes on, and give their own clothes to the household members.

The proprietor walks to and from, tears dripping from his eyes, and says:

"Thank you but no. We'll remain as we are. Why make ourselves into a laughing stock? We'll remain like this."

The soldiers get dressed, and the entire group bursts out laughing:

"Brothers, you look quite charming like this! What a wonderful costume party! Look in the mirror, and see how splendid you look!"

They look fantastic. One is dressed in a long black garment; a second in a tail coat; a third is attired in silk party clothes.

The merriment increases.

One of the commissars says to the owner:

"Nu? Get dressed! Get dressed!"

The owner refuses.

"Get dressed at once! All of you! No exceptions! That is, unless you want to go 'there!' You know what that means!"

The members of the house get dressed.

They laugh crazily when they look at each other.

They resemble circus clowns.

The two commissars rub their hands with glee, and explode with laughter. They are beside themselves with merriment.

"Oh! This is rich! How well-dressed you all look! Ha-Ha-Ha! Do take a look in the mirror! Oh my! Look at yourselves!"

The proprietor stands there in tattered clothes which are too short for him, with the face of a dead man.

He doesn't move.

"What? — You don't like them?! Take a look in the mirror how delightful you look!!!"

The man looks in the mirror.

His eyes are closed. —

Suddenly his daughter enters.

She stands for a moment, confused and upset, then bursts into hysterical tears. "Papa! Papa!"

The laughter stops for a moment.

One of the commissars goes up to her:

"Why are you crying? Do you think these people were dressed like this all their lives?!"

He looks at the men again, and again bursts out into fits of laughter. The laughter becomes louder and louder until it fills the house.

"Now, 'costumed images,' shake hands with each other!"

The "images" shake hands with each other.

"Good. Now let's go, lads!"

Just before they go, he bows ceremoniously to the owner's wife, saying:

"Gracious lady, be so good as to invite your husband to dance a waltz."

They leave.

Outside, I ask him:

"Why did you do this?"

"You're a fool!" he answers. "This is the whole point. What can be better than observing such a bourgeois costume party?"

He laughs, adding:

"Without this fun, this whole issue would be pointless!"

25.
Weaklings

There is a "line" in the courtyard of the only local cemetery.

The cemetery begins and ends with —a road. Actually, four intersecting roads — near the second-hand clothes market.

Each person with their dead dumped in a wheelbarrow or cart.

Each mother with her dead child on her shoulder.

The line is ordered, but crowded and jam-packed.

The grieving souls are filled with silent lamentation, and bitter envy;[60] envy of those who have already managed to enter the cemetery and bury their dead.

Meanwhile, the market owners are jesting:

"How much do you want for your jewelry?"

"You call that merchandise? It hardly weighs anything!"

"I'll pay the financial equivalent of all the food you have eaten in your life."

"I'll even compensate you for all the milk your baby has sucked. It's true that milk is expensive, but I'm no miser." —

I can't bear to listen anymore.

The words penetrate my heart like a stake, and from there ascend to the brain, darkening my sight with damp gloom.

I walk towards the "head" of the line with faltering steps and clenched teeth — towards the "head" of the cemetery line.

A group of weak old men are waiting there, next to the closed gate — one behind the other.

The crowd yells at them with choleric anger:

"What do they want here? Where are their dead? — Do they want to be buried alive?!"

I approach the cemetery gate, and hear a discussion between one of the old men and the *shammas*[61] who stands behind the gate and doesn't let them in:

"Where are your dead?"

"I have none! I myself am dead!"

"I have no time for games, old man. Dozens are waiting in line and you are wasting my time. Forward."

The old man doesn't move.

"Listen" he says with a blood-curdling cough, "neither I nor these others have come to play games."

He points to the other old men at the gate.

He adds:

"Listen to my few words. We have money. Each of us has several thousand (rubles)."

"What do you want? To buy dead bodies?"

"No. We want to buy burial plots for ourselves."

"Impossible! They're for the dead, not the living."

"Who is alive?" the old man says angrily, weak and moribund. "Who is alive? Me? Us?"

"Impossible! Leave at once!"

The old men go up to the gate, and take their "unfair" place in line (at cost to life and limb). One makes an angry movement, opens the worn clothes over his chest, and says tremblingly:

"Look! Look! Examine my heart! Is this a living heart?! Is it?! It hasn't beaten for 2 days already! — cruel man!!"

The first old man quiets and silences him.[62]

"Wait a minute!"

He turns to the *shammas* with words of admonishment.

"Hear my few words. The matter is very serious. We have a little money which we have recently saved. We haven't eaten: we saved a bit of money because we didn't have the strength to eat."

"Nu? Nu? So what do you want?"

"We want to enter and lie down until we die here. We'll pay for the plot and the grave. We'll lie in a secluded place for one or two days, and when we die, you'll bury us. Don't be cruel — you're a Jew, after all!"

The *shammas* laughs confusedly:

"Ridiculous. This is impossible! Buy yourselves some bread, so that you can live longer."

The old man bites his lip, his eyes become damp, he grinds his toothless jaw, and bursts into bitter tears:

"Thief! Murderer! Do you want us to die in the street, our bodies food for dogs? — God will repay you!"

He turns to go.

The *shammas* looks at him for a moment, then opens the gate.

"Nu, come, enter."

The weak old men enter with faltering haste.

The *shammas* points out:

"There, go there, under the tree."

The old men get to the spot as fast as they can, lie under the tree, and begin to shrink.

26.

A Thousand

The "Whites" have entered the city, and the owner of my house is walking around pale as death. — "Honored guests," the old man says shaking his head in terrible despair — "'Be honored, you honored and holy ones.'[63] Soon they will come and confiscate our home, and settle down here when it suits them to do so. The devil knows why our house is so attractive to these gentlemen. Why? I haven't got a clue."

He looks at me:

"Sir, you were not born in Russia: you are Austrian. Don't tell them that you are a Jew! Say that we have a 'goy'[64] living in our house."

"Impossible!"

"Why not? Why can't you say it, to rescue me? You must do it without hesitation. I'll tell them, that you are a goy, and you must please say nothing, please. Just a little[65] — any kind of help — I beg you! Who needs guests like these? Be honored — ."

Even before he has finished grumbling, a soldier enters.

He examines the apartment, and straightaway confiscates it.

"For our commanding officer![66] For his honor our commanding officer!" — he says as if to himself with excessive seriousness.

He turns to me:

"You must make yourself scarce today! This is the room where he rests! Do you understand?"

Of course I understand.

He leaves.

"Well?" — I ask the owner, "they didn't even ask me whether I am a goy or not."

"It doesn't matter," he says, "you will be a goy. Be honored, respected guests. I am very pleased to meet you."

In about a day's time, his honor the commanding officer arrives in all his glory.

"I am Officer Fischer!" — he introduces himself politely.

I look at him. Fisher? A German name?

"Pleased to meet you," I say and introduce myself. — "Please make yourself at home"[67] — I stammer, without taking proper note of what the owner of the house said to me before.

He looks at me with exaggerated politeness, and asks:

"Are you Russian, Sir?"

"No. I am Austrian."

"Ah! An Austrian? That is very, very pleasant. So you speak German?" (the owner of the house almost dances with joy. We will manage after all!).

"Of course!"

We speak German together.

I immediately understand from his words that he is from one the German settlements in Russia;[68] in his turn, he guesses that I am a former prisoner-of-war. He is nauseatingly polite to me, and very happy that we will be neighbors.

"We will live in peace" he says unctuously — "I'm sure that you haven't drunk a glass of wine for a long time. Don't worry, we have brought some with us. We even have some of your own wine with us — choice Tokay. Ah yes, I know that your officers are also experienced drinkers — is that not true? I, for example, drink for two: first as a German, then as a Russian."

Wine is consumed like water. The house buzzes with activity, noise and madness.

The owner's only attempt at "rescue" has succeeded. There is tumult in the city, with silent pogroms and "inquisitions." But, by comparison, the owner and his family are only too pleased with the courteous officer.

While we drink, I carefully observe my new "friend." His face is pale, damp eyes bulge out like onions, and his delicate, almost effeminate, hands — decorated with polished, sharp nails — tremble continuously.

Drink loosens his tongue.

"This isn't really drinking, sir" he says almost angrily. "I'll teach you what real drinking is! I drink for two! First as a German, then as a Russian! Wine and beer together! My German-Russian nature is characterized by three things: drinking, love of women and hatred of Jews. Ha-Ha-Ha!"

The dangerous question slips out:

"Why does his honor the commanding officer hate the Jews? I don't hate them at all!" — I say, laughingly.

"Why??" He answers seriously. — "We differ in this as well. You surely hate the Jews for economic, or other similar, reasons. Not me! Not me! Absolutely and definitely not!"

He pours out more wine, and adds:

"Do we hate the Jews? No, we don't really hate the Jews — what is there in them to hate? No, we simply want to destroy them — hate is not involved."

"Why is that?"

"Why destroy them? — actually it isn't that either" he added, now completely drunk. "Not destroy them — just 'fix' them a bit."

"What does that mean?"

"Yes. Fix them. I know that you don't understand this, my friend, but you must learn it from us. I beg forgiveness from you! You know so much, but you must earn this specific issue from us. I will explain it, briefly and succinctly."

He explains briefly and decisively, even though by now he is drunk as a skunk:

"There are all sorts of different races and nations in the world, and all have gradually developed in the course of time. Each in its own particular way, determined by way of life, blood, living conditions, and, more than anything else, country and climate. The Jews are the only exception to this rule. They also evolved, but mainly according to their country in the Middle East — Palestine, as you know. There, for example, they developed their dark eyes, black hair, sunburned skin, and — more than anything else — their crooked noses. Their nose is the…"

He mimics the Jewish nose with his hands.

"So?"

"So? Here is the fly in the ointment[69] with the Jews: After they lost their own land, they lived among us all this time — why do they still have their special characteristics? Why?"

"So?"

"So, we must fix them by removing all their physical characteristics. Ha-Ha-Ha-Ha! Isn't that so?"

"How do you do that?"

"How do I do it?"

He drinks some more, and says politely:

"I invite you to where the deed is done: to the 'Royal' theater."

I smell a rat. Terrible rumors have been doing the rounds about awful things done in the "Royal" theater.

In fact, the name "Officer Fischer" is associated with these inquisitorial deeds.

Now he is inviting me there.

"Should I go?" I ponder tremblingly.

I have no alternative. He is most emphatic about his invitation, which is almost a demand — if I don't go, he'll be insulted, and something tells me that will not be a good thing.

At night there is a knock on my door.

It's Officer Fischer.

"I'm waiting for you," he says seriously. "It is already 2.00 am. Please hurry."

I hesitate, and try to refuse; it doesn't do any good. I go with him.

Armed guards at the gate of the "Royal" open up a place of honor for us.

We have hardly entered the large hall, when I hear voices that make my hair stand up on end and strike me dumb — strange death rattles and high-pitched weeping.

"Well? How do you like our chorus?" he asks me.

"Excuse me, I can't — ."

"What a coward!" he says in his best officer style — "Please excuse me, I had no intention of offending or insulting you. But your behavior is unsuitable for an Austro-Hungarian officer."

He pushes me along into the middle of the theater.

I don't get a chance to see much. My head spins and my eyes cloud over, leaving me almost blind. He explains everything, showing me the poor creatures, writhing in agony.

"We have fixed this one's nose, and this one's mouth. This one has had some modifications made to his ears, and this one to his skull. We have removed this one's suntanned skin. What use is suntanned skin, living in Russia? This one over here — his back was bent over too much, so we stuck a pole into him, to straighten him up a bit."

I stand in shock for a moment, grope towards the door, and struggle outside.

His laughing voice echoes behind me:

"Ha-Ha-Ha! Ha-Ha-Ha! What a coward you are! You should be ashamed: an Austro-Hungarian officer who is a coward! Ha-Ha-Ha!"

He catches up with me at the gate, puts his arm around my shoulder, and says:

"Let's go back home! I see that you still have a lot to learn."

In all honesty, I should have known that I — am — a bit — of a coward.

At first, I cannot say a word: my mouth is dry and bitter.

After a few moments, I say:

"I request that you — truly — wretched — you are an intelligent man — as wise as if you were 120 years old — I implore you — why are you doing this?"

"Why?" he asks in complete seriousness — "Why?"

He stops suddenly in the middle of the street, next to me, and says:

"Tell me, sir, what little enjoyment can we derive from this accursed life, if we cannot at least get some pleasure from what we have just seen? Women and wine, wine and women!! Again wine and women, and women and wine!! Again and again and again!! I'm sick of the two already!"

When we return home, I myself request a little wine.

"With great pleasure!" he replies and pours a glass for me — "My pleasure! After that interlude, the wine will taste seven times sweeter. Na zdorov'ye! Prosit!"

"I have a request for you. Please promise me that you will agree to it."

"Please tell me."

"Stop doing these things."

"I'll explain it to you: I'll stop soon, but I have to fill a certain quota: I have to fix up 1,000 Jews — only 1,000 and no more, and I have already fixed about — ."

He takes out a small notebook and hands it to me.

The notebook contains a long list of Jewish names — about 900, if not more.

"This is nauseating!" I say to him — "Nauseating! It's enough to make one vomit and die!"

He adds:

"I am, after all, a *Regimentsherr*[70]! How many are in my regiment? A thousand, normally. Therefore I'll stop when I reach 1,000. Good?"

I go to sleep — my bed feels like a living grave.

After what seems like a few moments (it is already dawn!), the owner of the house enters with a mixture of panic and fear:

"SHHH! The Reds! The Reds are coming, Sir! He grabs my shoulders — are you a good Jew, Sir? We must keep you here until they come! — only you can do this! His subordinates like you very much. When they come to tell you something — you must listen for the news, and hold him here with wine!"

"Sir, if you don't catch that wild animal and hold him here, — you are no Jew!"

In two days' time, the commanding officer is in the hands of the Reds. When they catch him, I am amazed at what I see — he shows no sign of fear or excitement, his face isn't even pale. He is falling-down drunk, and keeps on stammering:

"It really is a great pity that you are going to kill me, 'comrades.' I was only one Jew short of making up my quota of 1,000: only one Jew short!"

He suddenly sees me:

"*You* know, sir! Comrades! This man knows. My job was to fix 1,000 Jews, and I am only one short! Only one!"

He turns to those transporting him, as if seized by silent madness:

"Comrades! I ask you: please just give me one more Jew, only one. You have so many — please!"

He goes on calmly to his execution.

27.
"A Joke"

The "civilized soldiers" of Denikin's Army walk around the streets in good spirits with trim, gleaming uniforms, laughing, but with eagle eyes:

They are on the lookout.

They are looking for enemies who remain loyal to the opposing side, and those who didn't have a chance to flee in time.

They look, and they find.

Nothing is easier than finding enemies.

Decent bread, human kindness, a place to rest, trains that work, a lasting compromise to stop this civil war — all these are hard to find. But finding enemies — that is a simple matter.

The enemy may be anyone who doesn't look right, for whatever reason.

There is one simple law for "enemies": immediate "elimination," without trial.

Trials are such boring things. By contrast, "elimination" is interesting and entertaining to observe.

The officers are haughty, and enjoy the joke.

They look for such jokes in the streets.

Very soon, they find their target: Look! An enemy!

This time, the victim is not Jewish, but a Russian tradesman, walking innocently on the sidewalk, bothering no one.

The officers stop him:

"Where in the hell are you going?"

Until a moment ago, the surprised victim hadn't given any particular thought to where he was going.

"Where am I going? — Just — for a walk. — "

"Ah yes," the officer responds, "you are going for a walk. You are obviously a layabout with nothing else to do but go for a walk. The day before yesterday you were still occupied with your holy work and didn't wander aimlessly around. But today — now that we are here, and your 'Tsar' has recoiled, and run back to Moscow, — you have been left without work."

"I don't understand. Which Tsar?"

"Which Tsar? What a question!! Why, your new kingdom's Tsar. His Majesty Tsar Trotsky, of course. — Please, just stand up against the wall."

The wretched man knows exactly what "against the wall" means: his face becomes ghostly pale, and his eyes fill with tears.

"I beg you, sir! I am a simple man. I was persecuted and driven away by the Bolsheviks as well! I didn't work with them! — Please, I beg you, no!"

"Enough with your wailing and grimacing. Against the wall!"

The man prostrates himself on the sidewalk. The officer kicks him, and says calmly:

"You can do this afterwards, 'comrade.' But first, against the wall with you! One, two!"

The poor wretch rises, stares with eyes devoid of all hope at each one of the officers in turn, pleading dumbly for a reprieve, all the while retreating slowly to the wall, with outstretched arms, dumb mouth and damp, bulging eyes.

"Not like that," — the officer corrects his stance — "turn this way a bit. That's it."

The poor wretch closes his eyes.

"That's not the way, 'comrade,'" the officer says. "Look straight into my eyes. Closing your eyes is not an option. Straight — into my eyes!"

The poor man opens his eyes.

"Hands straight at your side — calmly. Good, now you are standing in the prescribed way. Now."

One of the officers, from the group who has been standing observing everything with a smile of enjoyment, comes up to the "commanding" officer:

"Excuse me for a moment."

He goes up to the victim.

"I have a request for you, 'comrade' — "

The victim stands like a block of wood, understanding nothing. What is going on? The officer is asking something from *him*? A request? Before his death?

The officer shakes the man's hand, and says again:

"I have a request for you to fulfil. Will you do it for me?"

The victim blushes, his head moves to and fro, and he stammers with sudden sacred hope, writhing with happiness:

"Of course. Of course. With great pleasure."

"You will? Thank you very much!" says the officer. "In that case, I ask that, when you arrive in the world to come, you greet my grandmother for me. Good? Well then, thank you!"

He shakes the poor man's hand again, and then leaves, turns to the commander and, standing behind him, says with a smile:

"Thank you. Now you can go ahead."

Pistol shots. The poor man falls down dead. The entire group bursts out in merry laughter.

28

The Heretic[71]

He is one of my good friends, a pleasant lad, the kind of *yeshivah bokher* who "has gone to the dark side of profane culture." A brilliant scholar with as yet undeveloped literary talents. Avraham Welzer from Galicia.

In reality, he still lives in the period of the *Haskalah.*[72] His ideals are: Peretz Smolenskin, Mapu, the Josippon, Aristotle's "The apple," but above all the "Dessauer" Moshe ben Menachem ("Rambman") and his exegesis.[73]

His heart's desire is to "write" modern Hebrew, which he loves with an almost pathological intensity.

In the beginning, he was a "pure Zionist." After that, he felt the pain of the toiling masses, and became a member of *Poalei Zion.*[74]

"*Poalei Zion* is a lofty synthesis," he says to me happily. "Zion can only be rebuilt by the workers. It's a pity that I didn't feel this earlier. It's a pity about those who already gone and are no longer with us.[75] Each moment of our life is precious, and we must take the right path and not become trapped in dead ends from which there is no retreat.[76] I erred greatly until I arrived at this general rule: Zion and the workers go hand in hand. The Children of Israel were not members of the bourgeoisie when they left Egypt. The Torah says: 'and afterwards they will come out with great substance.'[77] These possessions did not belong to individual Jews, but to the all the Children of Israel. Here is the proof: they gave what they had, whether for the Holy Ark, or the golden calf. The bourgeoisie do not give! *Poalei Zion!* What is your opinion?"

I agree with him. It is too complicated not to.

"It's a terrible pity that they don't regard Israel as a separate nation" he says sadly. "They regard the Hebrew language as an abortion too. Without the Hebrew language, Israel cannot be redeemed. They may perhaps redeem the rest of the world — but not us."

He does not join them.

He approves of one thing that they do: those who were at the top are now at the bottom, and vice versa, as it will be when the Messiah comes. Those at the receiving end of the catastrophe are at now on top: they have been redeemed, and wield great power.

In the midst of the fulsome praise for redemption of the discarded at the bottom of the heap, his conversation inevitably arrives at the little village — filled with stifling darkness — where he was born and educated.

"I suffered greatly as a child, from the teacher's pinches and his strap. When I became a little older, I swore allegiance to our language, but this was absolutely forbidden. I was beaten senseless, everything was done to remove my desires[78] by those who walked in darkness and ignorance. Once they found Aristotle's 'Apple' in my hands, spat in my face, mocked me, grabbed me, put me on the table with my backside in the air, and beat me within an inch of my life. It took me days before the wounds began to heal.[79] — They all conspired against me and my highest aspirations. The worst culprits were the town rabbi and my father. The rabbi was a real monster: I only had to see him for my legs to buckle under me. He pushed me against the wall, stroked my cheeks, patted my head, and said: 'Nu, Avramele, do you still have evil thoughts? A good Jew must return to that question every day.

Come to me this evening.' — I went to visit him obediently, like a lamb to the slaughter.[80] When I entered his house, he went up to a small chest standing on the floor, took out the Josippon and Mendelssohn's 'exegesis,' which he had stolen from me two days before, and said: — 'this filth stays with me until you repent of it completely and absolutely. Then we will burn them together. We will destroy Moses Ben Menachem's book like chametz before Pesach.'[81] He gave me his nauseating hand to kiss, which I did, holding my nose. I left him weeping, but did not return repentantly. No! Oh, how I hate them all! All of them! All of them! The murderous rabbi, the *shochet*, the teacher, my father — all those good-for-nothings together!"

He stands in silent thought, and then says:

"Just one time in my life I should like to take revenge on them for my books — just once. It is not so much a matter of revenge, as to show them that these books are no less holy than their 'Zohar' of Rabbi Moses de Leon!"[82]

He pronounces these words mockingly, with bitter disgust.

The next day when we met, he has some news:

"I have joined the Red Guard!"

"How is this possible? What about the Hebrew language?!"

"That isn't important for the moment. The language is only a means to an end. The books are the main issue — they absolutely must be saved, to protect our heritage. Once and for all, we must make a clean break and say: 'Let there be light!'"

His eyes burn with fire:

"Redemption will never come until we purify our people from the pollution of book destruction, so that I have no need to turn my village into a wilderness of destruction, to protect my books from harm!"

I look at him. What a strange type! A soul who has arrived on the scene a little late: a young man who steps straight out of the books of Berdyczewski and Peretz![83]

His face is not the same as it was before: he is pale as a sheet with bloodshot eyes, as if he hasn't slept for days.

"You look a little ill" I say to him affectionately.

"On the contrary, I am finally recovering." He gets up, shakes my hand, and leaves.

The next day he visits me again and shows me something that he has written:

"Please read this, and tell me what you think of it."

I read what he has written: it's a sort of story, entitled (In Aramaic): "A public cemetery celebration[84] for Rabbi Shimon Bar Yochai."[85]

What a pleasant name!

The "book" turns out to be a disorganized jumble of thoughts from someone who didn't have the time to put them in order. If the word "content" could even be considered, it would be that of a confused mind, whose general goal is to marry the Zohar with the Angel of Death.

I tell him how bad his book is.

He is not upset, rises and says:

"If that is true, then I am not a real author, which frees me from writing literature, and allows me to actively make things happen. The darkness in that little village still asphyxiates me. My father is already dead, but the rabbi, and that miserable teacher, are still alive. It's my duty to save my books with my very soul!"

A few days later, that same Abraham Welzer comes to say goodbye to me and receive my blessing.

I am amazed at how he looks. A Red officer, dressed in uniform with a revolver at his hip.

"We are leaving," he said with confidence and joy, — "the Red Army is on its way to Hungary. It's our duty to unite the two proletarian countries.[86] We are already on the Romanian-Galician frontier."

"Will you visit your own village?" I ask.

A moment's silence. Then he stands up straight, shoulders thrust out, and stretches, yawning happily:

"Ah-h-h, what order I will bring to that miserable place! Nu, goodbye."

He departs.

I don't hear his name mentioned for a while.

Until I read the following article in a Polish newspaper: "The Heretic":

"Red Army Officer Avraham Welzer has destroyed his home village of Hrushe in a most cruel way. When his unit entered the village, Welzer commanded all the Jews to gather around him. When they had done so, he started to abuse them especially the Town Rabbi Shlomo Lebovitz, in a revolting way. He made the rabbi dance naked in the street and then made him eat books, forcing him to recite the *She'hecheyanu* prayer[87]: after that, he buried him alive with a copy of the Zohar. He then gathered together all his late father's books, went to the cemetery, opened his father's grave, and reburied him together with the books. After he had beaten all the Jews there within an inch of their lives, he set the village ablaze and immolated himself."

29.
A Foolish Woman

Yesterday the Haydamaky[88] entered the town.

Everyone is terrified.

The Haydamaky are "at work" — they go from house to house, arrest the youth, lead them to the town park from where no traveler returns. If perchance they do come back, they arrive with limbs broken and smashed into pieces, loaded on cemetery wagons.

Meanwhile, the rescue committee sits on its hands in the town hall.

The Haydamaky are governed democratically: they are kind enough to allow the rescue committee to sit in the town hall, and save the victims — once they are dead. Family members inform the committee of those who have been arrested, but by the time the committee manages to move an inch or two — the victim is finished.

Three Haydamaky enter our home and the home of a neighbor. They ask about the neighbor's two sons.

Both are school students.

The two young men are strong as lions and tender as young flower shoots.

The Haydamaky "request the pleasure" of the two young men's company.

"Please be so kind as to come with us: it is only routine and will only take a minute."

The household members fall at the Haydamakys' feet, kissing their feet, offering them money, possessions, anything. The Haydamaky answer with charming smiles:

"Please excuse us, but how foolish you are being. What are you afraid of? Who will put even a hand on your young men? Don't we know that they are still high school boys? We know who are Communists and who are not. You are the exact opposite of Communists: you are Zionists. Nothing bad will happen to you at all."

The mother weeps, clutching at their legs.

Again, they smile:

"A woman remains a woman! How foolish this mother is! We won't even raise our little finger to your sons! We would never raise a hand against Zionists! Why would we?"

The mother is momentarily encouraged:

"Truly — you are — please excuse me — truly — Am I not a foolish mother? But these two sons are all I have in my life — please excuse me — I believe you — I ask you to — ."

"Thank God you finally believe us: please excuse us but how foolish mothers are! It's as if you think we will eat your boys alive! A short routine visit, and then we will return them to you without a single hair on their head harmed."

They turn to the youths:

"Are you also afraid, lads?"

"We — are not afraid at all. Only mother is afraid." —

"If that is so, come — let's go."

They depart.

The mother collapses onto the sofa and mumbles some kind of whispered prayer.

I run to the rescue committee.

Fifteen minutes pass —

Thirty minutes pass. —

The mother runs wildly through the street, roaring like a crazed lioness.

They find her sons in the town park.

They are both dead: smashed and broken, lying in large puddles of blood.

The mother has gone mad.

She screams, bellows, kisses the blood, and bites herself.

Another Haydamak appears, leading a young man.

The woman looks at him with terrified, bloodshot eyes.

The words choke in her throat and she stammers:

"But you said — didn't you say — that they would return home? — What have you done? — What? — What?!" — "And why?!" —

The Haydamak turns to the young man he has brought along:

"What do you think about this foolish woman? What is she yelling about? Did we not return them home, as promised? Tell me — is your mother also as foolish as this?"

I stand to the side, a bitter, nauseating taste in my dry mouth.

I run back to the rescue committee.

Suddenly — I hear a shot.

I hurry back to the place.

The youth lies dead.

He is the third.

The crazed woman drags the corpse to her two sons' bodies, collapses on all three, and bites their bodies.

I, dressed in my Austrian uniform, go up confusedly to the Haydamak, and mumble some question or other, without even hearing what I am saying.

The Haydamak looks at me and smiles:

"Eh — Austrian — Tell me: are there such foolish Jewish women where you live as well?"

I lean against the tree, and darkness covers my eyes.

30.
The *Almaz*[89]

"Oh apple, apple[90]
Where have you rolled?
Have you boarded the *Almaz*?
You will not return from there alive, Selah!"
A hymn to abomination.

Few cities in the world are as immersed in laughter and joking as beautiful Odessa. Mother Odessa, the promiscuous whore, always, always happy and joyful. I wasn't able to see it during the pre-war decade, the glory days when Odessa, Imperial Harbor of the Black Sea Fleet, was filled with ships from many nations laden with the bounty of the earth.[91]

Ah, no: I was forced to see it when it was already torn and used, its harbor ruined and desolate, with no goods coming in or going out.[92]

But even in such a sorry state, Odessa is still "drunk with joy and laughter:" this has remained from its golden age. Nothing can harm it: economic warfare, bandits, famine, plague, revolutions, corpses in the streets, people dressed in rags — Odessa still jokes and laughs.

No city does biting national "gallows-humor" better than Odessa.

If anyone were to collect all the anecdotes from Odessa during the revolution and the recent time of troubles, the world would be presented with a classic horror book, laughing through convulsions of hellish suffering.

But still laughing.

The laughing is typically Jewish laughter: a gourmet dish of songs and melodies, basted with tears.

The subject of one of these songs is a version of the well-known Ukrainian (Russian) folk-song:

"Oh apple, apple." —

Even the word "Almaz" provokes terror. Before the war, the *Almaz* was a ship in the Tsarist Navy. It acquired the beautiful name "Almaz" (precious stone, diamond) after the revolution.[93] When the Bolsheviks dealt with their enemies after the Civil War, the ship was used for military tribunals, to deal with those who, for an entire generation, had cruelly tortured the intelligentsia, especially the Jews.

A certain governor, whose task was the removal of Jews without residence permits from Odessa; a certain officer who determined which young Jewish girls had yellow (prostitute) cards, without which it was not permitted to obtain a residence permit and attend school; a certain professor who, during his lessons, abused his Jewish pupils so cruelly, that a few committed suicide.

These, together with other members of the bourgeoisie, were the victims of trials on the *Almaz*. Sentence was swift and simple: a stone was tied around the condemned's neck, and he was tossed into the sea.

So, "anyone who boarded the *Almaz* never returned from it (alive), Selah!"

When I arrived in Odessa, the "*Almaz* club" was still very much alive, and their song was heard at all merry gatherings. Of course, in Odessa — all gatherings are merry, even if they commemorate catastrophic events.

But when I asked about details of the *Almaz,* peoples' hair stood on end from fear.

They were unable to tell me anything. It was as if they were struck dumb.

But they did sing — the song was intoxicating: it was the cause of endless and amazing fun. But not the background to it.

Once I got up in the morning and naively started to sing the song out of habit, because I had heard it so often before. Suddenly a young Ukrainian woman almost attacked me, with a terrible angry cry:

"SHH! Don't you dare! Aren't you ashamed of yourself?!"

It was my landlady's maidservant.

At a convenient time, I asked her to tell me something about this. The young woman agreed. Her face became distorted with pain, and she said, in restrained agony:

"I lost my husband in the clutches of those evil creatures. My dear husband, whom I love. He is not a human being anymore, but has become a living corpse."

She sighed, and continued:

"When the Red Army left the city and the Whites entered, all the victims' relatives came to search for their dead in the sea: amongst them was the rich landowner Gorbonov, looking for his son. When he found out that his son was amongst those drowned at sea, he offered a 1,000 ruble reward for anyone who could retrieve his son's body. We were living in great poverty at the time, and my husband took it upon himself to dive down and find his son's body according to signs his father gave him. A boat was made ready, he entered the water, and I waited for him on it. After a very few minutes, a loud call was heard from my husband above the water, frightening the people from bringing him out of the deep water. When he came out, he violently tore off his diving mask: when we saw his face and his eyes, terror struck all of us. Horror! Panic! His eyes were popping out of his head, it was as though he were struck dumb; on seeing me, he embraced me with terrifying fear, and whispered: 'Veruchka! Veruchka! To the church! Take me to the church! Quickly!' All questions were useless — what on earth was going on? Again, he said abruptly: 'To the church!' We ran to the church like madmen (before this happened, he had never prayed properly!). He bowed, fell on his face and burst out in wailing prayer. He prayed like this, as if to himself, for a long time and when he got up felt a little better. After we arrived home he asked for some vodka (he had never been drunk before, only a little alcohol for medicinal purposes). He told me: 'You know what, my Veruchka? — they are all praying there! They are all praying in the depths of the sea. But not like us. They are praying upside down: I swear by my life, with their heads below. Their legs sway this way and that, like Jews praying. It is too terrible for words, how they pray. It is absolutely horrible, how they move this way and that, praying! Horrible! Horrible!'

He burst into tears.

I understood at once and said to him: 'Obviously, Piotr, obviously their heads are below: heavy stones have been tied around their necks, which pull their heads down, with legs above, moving in the water. So why are you so terrified?'

'How can I not be terrified?' the poor, frightened man said. 'Dead people are praying, standing on their heads. I recognized a railway official praying the same way, moving, moving — .'

I calmed him down, silenced him, gave him more to drink, but he ate nothing — indeed he hasn't eaten anything for the past month, and has become skin and bone. Oh, oh, what has happened to us! *Almaz! Almaz!*"

She bursts into bitter tears.

After a moment she continues:

"Please come and see how he sits and drinks, looking but seeing nothing. He sits like this for days and weeks, without moving. Only sometimes, at night, he tries to stand on his head and then he falls over onto the floor and groans."

I see a young workman sitting like a heap of bones, staring silently into space. When asked something, he replies in a half-hearted tone, as if to himself:

"They are praying, praying under the *Almaz*. Their suffering must be too heavy to bear, so they pray, they pray." —

"O apple, apple — ."

31.
The Gift

I met him for the first time in Kiev, when I returned from Siberia. At the time he was a Haydamak, and I, a poor prisoner of war, an "Avstrietz." During the "silent pogroms," he had a very unique job: plucking out beards. His goal and ideal was not murder for its own sake — but rather plucking out Jewish beards. He explained it to me with classic Ukrainian simplicity; there is no greater pleasure than plucking out a Jewish beard!

Neither my friendship with him, nor his with me, stopped him from doing this. He laughed about it drunkenly, with an air of superiority:

"What a simpleton you are, Avstrietz! Try plucking out a beard for the first time, and you'll see what fun it is!"

I meet him again in Odessa: now he is a junior commissar. He is very happy to see me, leans over, and whispers the question in my ear:

"Are you a Communist?"

I answer carefully:

"But you already know that I am an Austrian!"

"Yes, I know. Are you still protecting Jewish beards, as you did before?"

"Are you still plucking them out, as you did before?"

He laughs, and says with sad seriousness:

"It's a little difficult now. At the moment I can only 'cash them in' and send them to the next world, not pluck out their beards.[94] I am cashing in the entire Jewish bourgeoisie at the same time."

He thinks for a moment and adds:

"But just cashing them in is a very boring business, and I seldom get a chance to pluck out beards: only when those sons of bitches are not looking — "

He looks around carefully, then takes a skein of tangled black, yellow and white hair out of his pocket.

"Here."

I shudder.

"Give it to me as a gift, my friend."

"No, my Avstrietz! I will not give you this: anything else, but not this. This is a gift for my young lady in Darnitsa — I promised it to her."

32.
The Game

Famine has strangled the city. Ghostly shapes flit around the streets, searching faces to see whether anyone has had anything to eat. Soup made from tan bark has become a diet staple. Ordinary people cannot obtain the slightest drop of oil, or pinch of salt.

Food and their components are still found in the villages, but the farmer doesn't share them. He goes out to kill something or other for himself and his family to eat, and does not give anything away.

The streets of Odessa are full of emaciated shadow-people, skin and bone, thin as sticks.

Cases of cannibalism are mentioned in hushed tones. This one and that has butchered his wife and children.

I meet my friend the kindly philosopher-scholar Ilya Markovich Veryan. He still has something to eat because he works, lecturing and speaking for the ruling authority. He is the exception to the rule, sharing his food with the half-dead.

We walk softly though the quiet streets and talk of God, of Spinoza's "Logos."[95] Does Logos wish this? Does "He" really take pleasure from it all? What is His goal? If it is a game, it is truly a terrible one.

We suddenly see two dead dogs lying one on top of the other.

I look and see: it is as if the two cadavers are stuck to each other. — "they died with a kiss."

Veryan leans down and examines them more carefully (he is also a noted physician-biologist).

"They died of hunger, — of hunger," he says shaking his head, "while they were copulating. Strange — ."

God's word is a game — a bad joke.

33.
"Love"

I have a peculiar type of luck: The Whites believe that I am a Hungarian officer, and the Reds that I am a Hungarian Communist. Nothing I can say can convince them that I am simply a Zionist, who wants to immigrate to the Land of Israel.

"What nonsense you are talking! We know that you are a Hungarian[96] officer! Here — have some vodka with us!"

"You aren't a Zionist — you are a Hungarian Communist! There are no more Hungarian officers left."

Charming Russian naïveté.

By this merit, I am shown, in turn, the horrors that both have perpetrated. A counter-revolutionary comrade shows me the Cheka's[97] bloody work. A comrade from the Cheka shows me the exact opposite. They use the same chamber of horrors: the cellars of 8 Yekaterina Street. They are kind enough to let me in, and explain everything. Hatred gives rise to unimaginable cruelty.

I will not try to describe what I see; it is beyond the abilities of my poor pen, and not for human eyes to see or read.

I go down the iron steps — it is like a descent into hell.

The lowest step is broken, and moves under my feet; I almost fall. The bannister is also broken.

Why are these broken?

My friend explains:

"This is the most terrible place of all. Here, the victim grabs on with all his strength and doesn't want to go down further, under any circumstances. Sometimes his hands must be cut off. The last step." —

My hair stands on end.

The strong, coppery smell of blood nauseates me, and makes me want to vomit.

He takes me into one of the "rooms," where the prisoners wait to be killed. I see graffiti on the walls:

"I want to live! I don't want to die!"

"I haven't done anything wrong!"

"Borya, don't forget me!"

There are many others. But the most common one, repeated over and over again, is:

"I want to live!"

I am struck dumb, faced with the riddle of life and death.

My friend interrupts my thoughts:

"Look here!!"

I see disgusting, sexually explicit, pornographic graffiti, with matching images.

"Look, these miserable, filthy swine!" My guide into hell curses, "They're on their way to death and decomposition, but still fixated with sex!"

I look, observe, read — and begin to understand the riddle of life and death.

I go outside, as if in a drunken stupor.

34.
Art

He is a young and talented artist of about 25, who paints
with oils, water and charcoals: excellent landscapes as well as
people. His special favorite is portrait painting, and
depictions of the human face, which sometimes reach great
depth and understanding.

He shows me his latest works. I enjoy them greatly; he
really is an outstanding artist.

He shows me two study paintings: they both have the
same name: "suffering."

Exceptional work of the modern school. His technique is
still incompletely developed, but the works are deeply
intuitive and unusually perceptive. They remind me of
Dostoyevsky.[98]

"Why don't you leave this hell-hole? You should travel
overseas to perfect your art: a brilliant future awaits you! Run
away from here, my friend!"

He lights a cigarette, inhales deeply, and says calmly:

"No. Firstly, I cannot. I am a stand-in for an important
service and they will not allow me to leave."

"Which is that?"

"I am the Deputy Commissar for Death."

I look at him; he is the deputy executioner.

I stare at him; he continues:

"I see you are surprised. Why do I need to travel out of
the country? There is no other place where I could learn
what I am learning here; it makes all other schools of theory

worthless and obsolete. That is the reason why I am doing this; to learn."

"But how?! I don't understand!"

"Look at these two paintings, and you will see. One is the face of a bourgeois, the other of a proletarian."

"Did you kill them?!"

"No. I am not a murderer. After great difficulty and effort and a large amount of protektsiya, I succeeded in being appointed Deputy Commissar for Death."

I look at him but do not understand.

"What don't you understand? Each time they are taken out to be killed — I improve my techniques. I aim my revolver at the condemned person's face, his eyes, his mouth, his heart — and observe the different facial contortions. Which other artist has such an opportunity? Look at the difference between these two paintings. — "

I look at them again. What do I really see?

35.
Criticism

The Commissariat for Enlightenment has, after much difficulty, decided to permit an operetta to be performed. Up to now, this musical form has been forbidden by the Reds, because it is regarded as bourgeois art. But, finally, they have issued a performance permit. It is, of course, free. Before it begins, the commissar ascends the stage, in an effort at self-justification:

"Even though it is bourgeois art, coming here is better than visiting a whore-house. It satisfies the sexual urge without causing venereal diseases."

The operetta is called *Monna Vanna*.[99]

The performance is very good, enjoyed by all.

Monna Vanna appears on the stage, apparently naked: throughout the performance she presents only her arse to the audience.

"Turn around! Turn around and come nearer! We all want to have a good look!" the audience yells.

There is no escape. She has to show the officers her "wares." She turns to the audience, so that they can get a full frontal view. A disappointed moan arises from the audience, followed by yells:

"Get off the stage! Right now!" — she is dressed in an undergarment. "Get off the stage! Cheat!"

Monna Vanna is forced to disappear.

36.
Shame

Workers who have turned traitor have recently filled the ranks of the condemned, and are buried by prisoners belonging to the bourgeoisie, who must divide up their last rites amongst themselves. They are not worthy of being honored by the proletariat; nevertheless even though they were traitors, they were still workers — and the bourgeoisie must perform their own last rites.

One of my neighbors, a factory worker, was condemned as a traitor yesterday, and executed today by the Cheka.

I am surprised to see that fellow-workers, not the bourgeoisie, are taking him for burial.

His wife explains to me, weeping bitterly:

"The poor man submitted a special request to the Commissariat, that they not shame him by burying him like this: he should be buried by 'fellow-comrades,' not by the bourgeoisie. At first they refused, but I fell at their feet and implored them. Finally they gave in, but by that time the poor man was already dead! The poor man! He died in shame and disgrace! Oh, if only I would have known beforehand! I could have at least whispered it to him before he died! My poor husband! He died in disgrace!"

She weeps inconsolably over the shame.

37.
The Rulers

There is general famine. Thousands of workless, ravenous people mill about in the streets.

Roads are buried in a thick blanket of snow from last night's storm.

I go out and see: prisoners of from a camp for the bourgeoisie are slaving at clearing the streets. Sweat pours from their faces.

They are surrounded by a horde of the unemployed, staring at them.

One of the workers says to a diminutive bourgeois prisoner:

"Nu, are you enjoying your work? Now we have the upper hand."

The small man squints at him for a moment, and says: "Wait a bit. Soon!"

"Wait for what? What do you mean soon?" the worker asks.

"Soon, very soon you'll see."

The workers mock them insultingly, needling them and laughing at their hard work.

Suddenly there is a cry:

"Eat!"

The bourgeois immediately throw down their shovels, and their commissar guards distribute food: bread, herring, roasted potatoes — they eat. —

There is a sudden end to the laughing and joking. The workers stand with eyes popping out of their heads with longing, at the food and those who are eating it.

The diminutive bourgeois again squints at the worker and, mouth stuffed with food, asks:

"Now, comrade, who rules here?"

38.
Courtesy

The Whites have captured a "very dangerous Red." He is led forth in the road by an officer before a crowd, who accompany the "funeral procession," in a group.

But the prisoner, instead of going quietly, in trembling and fear of death as usual, smiles cheerfully and politely. He even speaks politely, as if he were inviting those accompanying him to a party.

One of the crowd yells at him, cursing and insulting him with every conceivable kind of Russian obscenity — but he answers with a soft smile:

"Why are you cursing, comrade? Why are you getting upset? Please calm down. It really isn't worth it, you know." —

"Shut, up, you son of a Red dog!"

"Thank you kindly, comrade."

"Your father is a dog, 'comrade,' and you are a son of a bitch."

"Thank you, comrade. You are quite right. He is a comrade as well; we are all comrades together."

The crowd bursts out laughing. The escort fires at the crowd:

"Leave this instant!"

The polite prisoner adds:

"Don't do that, comrade, they don't all need to leave. Why? This is a charming demonstration. If they want to look on, why not?"

The officer beats him with his whip — but the prisoner smiles:

"Thank you very much, comrade. Thank you very much."

The officer becomes surprised. The prisoner says:

"Why are you surprised that I do not despair, comrade? What is there to make me despair? To die? — It is a very good thing to die. Am I not right? A man has the privilege to die only once in his life, correct?"

"Listen to what this Red son of a bitch is saying!"

The surprised officer takes out a bottle of vodka and drinks, while walking. He drinks, beating the prisoner, who says:

"Lechayim,[100] comrade, lechayim! To your health!"

He doesn't seem to feel the whip at all.

The officer loses his patience, and screams:

"Up against the wall! Right here!"

Without even the necessity of a "trial," he pushes him against the wall of one of the houses, to finish him off, and thereby wipe the smile off his ugly kisser.

The prisoner is still smiling:

"Here? Good, comrade. With pleasure!"

Still smiling, he points to his heart and then to his head:

"Please, either here or there; whichever you wish, comrade."

The officer looks at the prisoner and his audience. By now, he is completely drunk. He points his revolver at the "comrade" and looks at the crowd, who mirror his look of surprise. The prisoner continues:

"Please, comrade, aim your revolver here. Shoot straight at my heart — or else here at my head," he says in sing-song fashion. "It really makes no difference to me: heart or brain, please."

The officer gnashes his teeth, prepares to fire — but once more the prisoner interrupts him, saying again: "please, comrade." The officer is nonplussed, shrugs his shoulders and looks at the crowd with questioning eyes:

"What in the hell is this? Has he gone mad?"

"I? Mad? God forbid! Of course I am not mad! I am a 'very dangerous Red!' Please kill me! Please!"

He uncovers his chest.

"Please, shoot right here!"

The officer goes right up to the prisoner, as if examining him carefully face to face. The "comrade's" smile become broader and broader until it turns into a burst of politest laughter.

"Please! Ha-Ha-Ha! Please! Don't be afraid!"

The officer looks at the prisoner, and spits in his face:
"Pfui!"

He walks away.

39.
Odessa

Odessa, city of eternal jokes.

Nothing can change that. Odessa is one of the merriest cities I have ever seen. If Berlin is the symbol of order, Paris of love, Leipzig of science, Munich of art and London of trade, Odessa is the symbol of joking and eternal anecdotes.

No amount of suffering and death — in all its different forms — can stop the jokes.

Famine gnaws at the city's innards like a cancer — and Odessa jokes.

Counter-revolutionaries and Chekists kill thousands of people — and Odessa tells stories.

The city changes control like a soiled shirt, from rightists to leftists, from leftists to bandits and from bandits to anarchy — and Odessa still laughs at everything. Its stories and anecdotes mock everything and everyone: Denikin, Trotsky, Makhno[101] and Mishka Japonchik[102] (secretary general of thousands of thieves and bandits), Jews, Russians, Ukrainians, the dead, the living — everyone, all together.

Instead of leftist or rightist ideologies, in Odessa anecdotes reign. The joke is the only determinant factor in arguments.

Because of this, when workers councils understood the danger posed by jokes — they aggressively banned them completely. Anyone caught joking or even telling a story is executed on the spot. This applies, even if the joke is not about the government.

A Jew relates:

"Why are the banknotes printed in all languages of the governing authorities — Russian, German, French, English, even Chinese — but not in Yiddish?" He answers:

"Because of the printer's modesty."

Because of this little anecdote — hinting that the workers are in reality governed and controlled by the Jews — the jokester pays with his life. A commissar deals him a mortal blow, and he collapses like a limp rug on the ground at the corner of Pushkin Street and Mala Arnautskaya.

All for no purpose. The anecdote is whispered around in trembling and fear of death — but it is repeated and repeated.

Had Juvenal been living in Odessa today, he would have written: *difficile est anecdotam non narare*[103] (it is difficult not to tell an anecdote).

I sit in a cabaret opened with government permission. The conférencier (master of ceremonies) tells typical Odessa jokes: the audience split their sides with laughter.

Only one commissar sits in the lodge, as if on hot coals. He moves back and forth, gets up as if he wants to leave the hall, but restrains himself and sits down again.

A new "narrator" arrives on stage, and the master of ceremonies reappears. However, no sooner has he opened his mouth than a revolver shot is heard, and the master of ceremonies falls down dead.

Confusion reigns. The corpse disappears behind the screens.

The commissar, who shot the man while seated, rises, bows to the audience, and says politely:

"Quiet, comrades!"

Then, facing the stage, he says:

"Please continue!"

One of the performers comes out and says:

"The respected audience surely does not know what happened here. The angels in heaven who arranged the revolution received a cabaret permit, but they didn't have a master of ceremonies." —

Laughter. The commissar claps. Seriously.

40.
Chametz[104]

All gold must be handed over to the authorities. Hiding it carries the severest penalties.

The fate of anyone caught concealing gold is sealed — "up against the wall!"

It makes no difference whether it is a wedding ring, a gold hook in a medical instrument, a gold earring found in a drawer, or the tiniest gold hair clip — death awaits all who hide gold.

Because possession of gold is as strictly prohibited as chametz on Pesach, they call Odessa "chametz."

A certain shoemaker's wife, who has been a member of the "Shashal" synagogue for the past 20 years, transgresses this order openly and in public; a gold tooth sparkles between her ruby-red lips. (Where in Heaven's name has she found lipstick in these times of shortages?)

This tooth has recently caused her a great deal of trouble. Everyone — including officials in different administrations — ogles it with covetous eyes.

"Have the thing pulled, damn it! Why put your life in danger?"

Apart from different "legal" governments, Odessa also has a government of "fancy-dressers:" thieves and bandits who fall upon passersby in public, strip them of their clothes, and leave them lying in the street in their undergarments.

Many of the fancy-dressers are officers. And a gold tooth in the ruby-red-mouth of a pretty woman less than 40 years of age is certainly a potent distraction.

The Reds put an end to all the different kinds of fancy-dressers within 24 hours. They tolerate neither riots nor theft. The thief, the rioter/pogromist and the bandit — all are punished by zealots.[105]

But a gold tooth in the mouth of a shoemaker's wife is very annoying.

Annoying to both her and her husband.

"Remove the chametz from your mouth!" the shoemaker says to her, while trying to repair my worn out black shoes.

"I thumb my nose at them!" the pretty woman says, teeth laughing from between her plump lips.

"I evaded the fancy-dressers, the various robbers and bandits, Denikin, Makhno, Tyutyunnik[106] and innumerable others — with God's help I will evade them as well."

"But you will never escape from the 'law!'"

"What kind of a law is that, that forces me to have a tooth pulled?"

Once, a "neutral" commissar (one who succeeds in working for every government, no matter which it is) says to her:

"Hey, Madam. It looks as if you value your tooth more than your life!"

I finally lose my patience with her as well:

"Why on earth do you keep that dangerous chametz in your mouth? Get rid of it, for God's sake!"

The woman smiles sweetly:

Her sweet smile gives me the answer to my question: half of her beauty lies in that tooth: so why do without it?

But the danger that centers around that accursed tooth increases rapidly. The shoemaker's house is searched countless times and, after each search, everyone remembers the yellow gold in her mouth.

The Reds are getting ready to leave the city.

The pretty woman laughs: "I have got rid of them as well!"

The city is noisy: the tumult increases hourly. In the dark night, we do not know who is in charge. The war becomes ever more bitter.

The next morning, the pretty woman is found half dead, her mouth oozing blood.

The law has pulled her tooth out.

"It must have been a Jewish commissar!" the joke goes round the city. "A Jew has removed the chametz.[107] Pesach is coming!"

41.
The Tax

There is no separate law for children. If the father or mother have transgressed and escaped justice, the child is condemned to death, as a warning to the parents.

The child of a leatherworker who works in his enclosure has put his parents in mortal danger, by hiding a gold coin amongst his toys.

A 5 ruble coin.

The mother implores him in vain, to give her the dangerous coin, destroy it, or hand it over to the authorities.

The child at once says: "No!"

"Why are you surprised?" — the mother explains. "He has painstakingly, and with great effort, been collecting small coins, one by one, for more than 3 years to exchange for this 5 ruble piece. He is waiting for someone travelling to Israel, so that he can send the coin with him."

The child has been collecting coins for the Jewish National Fund.[108] When he arrived at the amount of 5 rubles, he exchanged the coins for the gold piece.

Now cruel and evil men want to steal his sacred fortune from him.

I explain to the boy the dangers of keeping it. He makes an innocent face, in an effort to deceive me:

"It's all lies. I don't have anything. I had a coin once, but I exchanged it for smaller amounts of money a long time ago, and bought various things with it."

The young boy's mouth lies, but his eyes give him away.

Searches in the city go on and on.

The parents walk around as if drugged. They implore, explain, threaten, the wife weeps, the father beats the boy. He cries and says:

"What do you want from me? I don't have anything, so what can I give you? Can I give you nothing?"

The mother weeps, the father beats him, but the boy remains silent.

The searchers arrive. The man in charge knows about the coin. Someone must have informed on the boy.

The man starts with words of admonishment, which change to rebuke, and then to threats. — Finally, he looks the boy straight in the eyes — and, suddenly, slaps him cruelly and violently across the face with all his strength. — The boy stands without moving a muscle — the side of his face that has been slapped is reddened, the other side is as pale as a sheet.

Blood oozes from his obstinate mouth.

The mother falls at the man's feet, kissing his boots. The father implores:

"Here! For the price of this coin, take my work tools: they are all that I own. Take our beds, our table, but in the Name of God leave our son alone!"

"Yasha, Yashinka darling," the mother weeps, clasping the boy's legs, — "my only dearest son! If you have the coin, for God's sake give it to him! Oy vavoy! Look at all the blood! Oy vavoy!"

She prostrates herself on the ground, as if dead.

Everyone present trembles, begs, weeps, persuades, walks back and forth.

But only two people stand like trees rooted in the ground: the searcher and the boy.

Two fighting cocks, looking each other in the face without saying a word.

The man looks at the boy again, his eyes narrow slits:

"So? Where's the coin?"

"I don't have one."

"I'll give you other coins. Where is the gold coin?"

"I don't have one." (The boy knows that the coins they want to give him are valueless).

"You don't? Well, take that!"

He slaps the boy across the face, even harder than before.

The mother faints.

The boy stands, his legs move slightly as if he is about to fall — suddenly he leaps at the man, scrapes his face furiously with his nails, plucks and scratches like a crazed wildcat, wraps his arms around the man's neck and bites him in the face. The man grabs him and hurls him bodily against the wall like a rag doll.

"You miserable little son of a bitch!" the man says, smoothing his hair and wiping the blood off his face.

He departs with his friends.

When I go to visit the little, injured patient two days later, he whispers to me with a serious little smile:

"Yesterday I handed the tax (as he calls it) to one of our acquaintances, who is going to Israel. He escaped via Romania."

He adds:

"Now they can search till hell freezes over, and I'll tell them the truth: I have sent the money to the Land of Israel."

42.
Him

A unique personage lives in Odessa. The entire city trembles with unexplained excitement in the hope of seeing him. Everyone longs to at least catch a glimpse of him from afar; all speak about him with nauseating fear and trembling horror, and all would give up a day of their wretched lives for one glimpse of his terrible face.

Rumor upon rumor abounds about this terrible man; no one has yet managed to see him, and he is spoken of in conjectures, fabrications and riddles.

But no one has been lucky enough to see him.

And no one knows his name.

They guess in hushed whispers.

They say that he is as dark as a gypsy.

They say that he is ruddy, with bulging eyes.

He is always drunk, and doesn't know his right from his left.

He is given whatever his heart desires.

Every day he has several women.

The poor souls!

Never has there been a king, prima donna, rich man or murderer, whom people have wanted to see more than this one man.

He is referred to by the people as "Him."

He is the executioner of the Cheka.

All my life I have had the good fortune of not using loyalty to authority — for example Reds or Whites — to obtain any particular favor. I am happy not to be considered suspicious by any side in this particular conflict. But even I am seized by the whole city's curiosity to see "Him." I once got to see the Hungarian executioner Bali "at work": he was a parasite on society who was paid very well indeed. And when did he "work?" Once in a blue moon.

But this man works on a wholesale basis day and night: everyone together.

I ask one of the important commissars. He replies:

"He has been a little ill during the past few days. Come with me to the convalescent sanatorium."

This is the first time I am able to enter the sanatorium courtyard. I hear tyrannical yelling from the inside it sounds like someone shouting out orders.

"'He' is yelling," the commissar says, "but it doesn't matter; he always yells. I'm not afraid of him; he really is a good man, who wouldn't hurt a fly. You'll see how I talk to him. We have known each other for a long time, and he really is a good person."

We enter: the hall reverberates with the "good man's" yelling.

I will not even try to describe how and what he is shouting: the Hebrew language does not contain such foul obscenities.[109] Even for Russian — a language well-versed in cursing — the style and language are remarkable.

Some of the people's conjectures are correct without their knowing it: he really does have a ruddy complexion, with bulging eyes.

The man leaves an indelible impression on me.

After the yelling — audible even from outside — he lies on the sofa and breathes heavily.

A man red as fire, with bright blue eyes and red eye-lashes. Eyes popping out like a newly-butchered calf, moving round and round as if searching for something in the air and not finding it.

His red hair is wild and damp.

He is big, fat and very strong.

I get the feeling that some sort of disease is eating at his powerful body, which is gradually atrophying and rotting inside.

Strong drink, and drugs such as cocaine and morphine, are devouring his body.

The commissar goes up and greets him.

"Sit down, comrade!" — he replies.

His voice is hoarse, but still strong; like a grating double bass.

The commissar introduces me:

"My friend, a comrade from Austria. A Hungarian Communist."

His tired eyes look at me for a moment:

"Please, sit down, comrade!"

He asks:

"Did you come to visit the 'poor bastard?'"[110]

I regain my composure, and say to him with great respect:

"I have seen Lenin, Trotsky, Lunacharsky,[111] and I have a friend in the Moscow Central Committee. I wanted to meet you as well."

"OK then, take a look" he says with a hint of irony "I'm something to see, am I not?"

His Russian language skills leave a lot to be desired.

"I'm something to see, right?" he continues, "'The Death's Head Commissar!' I am not a hangman, comrade! I am not a hangman! I am a Death's Head Commissar!"

(Excitement makes his voice louder: a kind of restrained anger, which gradually turns into a powerful roar).

"Death's Head Commissar! Commissar of all Commissars! Without me these is no revolution! Everyone is against us! They should all stand before me once in their lives, so that I can deal with them!"

He pours out vodka and hands me a glass.

"Drink, comrade!"

"Thank you very much, but I have drunk too much today already."

"Drink, I tell you!"

.....

"Do you understand me or not?"

I take a sip of the strong vodka. He drinks it in one gulp, and slams the empty glass down onto the table. His eyes bulge even more.

"Apparently you are too spoiled! Drink some more!"

The commissar — who has in the meanwhile secretly emptied his own glass under the sofa — saves me: "He is ill — he suffered terribly during the war, and after that became a prisoner of war."

"Aha!" — he says, — "he was in the war! I also suffered badly during the war. Those fucking sergeants and corporals who beat me and spat in my face. Now I am getting my own back on them! They spat in my face!! Right in my face! — Do you understand? And they punched me in the face as well! Here (an obscene curse)! They made me drink piss! Piss! — Do you understand?! Piss!"

He snarls and aims a big gob of spittle on the wall. On the wall, not on the floor.

He sits tiredly, and says, as if to himself:

"Only one thing counts in this world — death. — I'm not a murderer or robber, but death is a great thing. A very great thing. Revolution — that means death! Death! (obscene curse). Death to all! To all! All I need is a warrant — and then I fix them all! All of them!"

He gets up, looks at me, and strikes me on the back.

"You were in the army! A courageous man! You suffered as well. They must have spat in your face as well! Are you — are you — a Hungarian?"

"Yes, I am."

"I am a Lett from Latvia![112] The Tsar gnawed both at us and at Kaiser Franz Joseph like a mad dog: he wanted to devour us whole! (He snarls ferociously again). That fucking Tsar — that son of a bitch! His wife the whore as well! I am the Death Head Commissar! I'll put an end to all royalty! I'll finish them off like the mongrel dogs they are! There is only one thing!" —

He snarls again — sits down, and gets up again as if in deepest agony

"I'm just upset about one thing! One thing! Why didn't they give him to me to finish off? Why??!"[113]

His anguished cries make the whole building shake.

The commissar gets up, indicating to me that it is time to go.

"He" feels that we are about to leave, grabs me, and says:

"Don't leave! You cannot leave until you answer my question why they handed the Tsar and his whore over to someone else?![114] Why, damn it?! I don't believe that they killed them!! I just cannot believe it! The bastards were bribed, and released him! You understand? — They released him! Give me the Tsar! Give him to me, fuck it! You bastards! I'll crush their skulls into bloody pulp! The Tsar!"

His screams turn into hoarse wheezing and then into a doleful sigh. He collapses on the sofa, and weeps bitterly:

"The Tsar is alive! The fucking Tsar is still alive! — He is alive, that son of a mongrel whore! — Why didn't they hand him over to me to get rid of?' The Tsar! — the Tsar!"

He weeps like a wretched child.

We steal outside without his noticing.

Outside, the commissar tells me:

"He is a good man — he only wants the Tsar! What can we do? Where can we find a Tsar for him? He gets whatever his heart desires: nothing can be withheld from him. But this business of the Tsar is eating him up alive, and that is the one thing we cannot give him."

What a pity.

43.
The Stockbroker

"How much money do you have, sir? It doesn't matter, I'll put up ten times more than you have. Business is business. This is a good opportunity to make money, not so?"

This is the signature tune of the stockbroker, known throughout the city.

He himself is not from Odessa, but from Petrograd; he came here after the Bolshevik Revolution. In Petrograd, he was an important stockbroker, and at one time took part in the most important deals in Europe. An opportunist and risk-taker of the first magnitude.

The revolution forced him out of Petrograd to the nearest city and, from there, further and further away, until finally he arrived in Odessa.

From Odessa he tried unsuccessfully to go overseas.

The more he was plagued by financial and ethical troubles — the more confused his mind became.

In the beginning, he dealt with large speculations; these became smaller and smaller, until they disappeared completely.

Now, completely unhinged, he "continues" his stockbroking activities, walking around and talking to himself.

Sometimes he earns a few pennies — but instead of buying food, he secretly buys overseas newspapers forbidden by the authorities, "participating" in large deals in large local stock markets. He reads the newspapers surreptitiously, and "develops strong business connections" with the reports. He talks, and seriously and self-importantly discusses issues with them. He "buys" highest quality gems, and "sells" them at a large "profit." He leases large sections of land in Holland, Germany and Hungary, also forests and large lakes teeming with fish.

However the poor wretch has, in recent days, despaired even of these activities which (of course) bring him no profit at all, and has started to transact real business, which will at least bring something in.

His new business consists of the "stock market of life," as he calls it. He identifies someone of importance in the city, and "invests" him in the market; will the authorities kill him, or not?

When the Red are in charge, he "invests" an important member of the bourgeoisie; under the Whites, he "invests" in whether they will carry out anti-Jewish pogroms in a certain village or town. (He has, it appears, stopped thinking about the possibility of leaving the country — even under the Whites, when he really could have left).

"How much money do you have, sir? Do you know this or that member of the bourgeoisie? I will place 100 rubles on his life: how much will you invest?"

Or:

"There are fifty Jews in this village. Will there be pogroms, or not? How much do you invest?"

One cloudy day, he too is brought to the "last station." They have found some Romanian banknote or other in his possession, after the strict order against any foreign exchange speculations. — They don't believe that he is mad.

On the way to execution, he asks those he meets on the way, and those escorting him:

"How much money do you want to invest on my execution? Will they or will they not kill me? Do you say no, sir? In that case, how much will you invest on my life?"

44.
Electricity

We walk around for several days, drained of hope. Then, H. N. Bialik and Mosheh Kleinman[115] arrive from Moscow with a permit for us to leave Russia and travel to the Land of Israel![116] This is, at least for me, the eighth wonder of the world. Trotsky himself could not receive a permit to leave Russia at this moment.

We travel on the Greek ship *Anastasia*. It is the size of a large rowboat, and every wave swamps the deck, drenching us. No matter — we are travelling, from darkness into light.

In Kushta (Istanbul) lunch is sent for us onto the ship.

We stand astonished, before a feast fit for kings:

Chicken soup.

White bread.

Vegetables.

Roasted meat.

Cakes.

Fruit and wine.

Soda water.

A white tablecloth with napkins.

We see, but do not believe.

There are toothpicks on the table, to clean between our teeth.

Great Lord above — is this all possible?

"How does one use these?" asks A. Druyanov. [117]

"Why is there no 'booklet of instructions' on how to use them?" — a second writer asks.

Bialik says: — "I want to see who of you dares sit down and eat all this food!"

He sees: Not even a gnawed morsel of bone remains on the table after we have finished.

Where are the toothpicks?

Even they have disappeared.

They send a carriage pulled by splendid horses, to take us into the city.

On the way, I see stores full to bursting with rich fruit, and the plumpest vegetables I have ever seen.

Stores selling gold and silver ornaments.

In one shop-window I see starched and ironed white shirts. —

"Why are you weeping?" — Mrs. Bialik asks me.

There really are tears in my eyes.

I stand at the entrance of the magnificent hotel, and look at the beautiful furniture in the spotless room.

My girlfriend[118] falls onto the soft sofa, sinks her head into the soft pillow, and weeps with joy.

The blinding sun covers the room with its radiance.

I switch all the electric lights on.

The large clock booms in a dignified, smiling tone:

"One — two — three." —

Notes

[1] Ahad Ha'am (Asher Zvi Ginsburg) (1856–1927), Hebrew essayist, and one of the foremost pre-state Zionist thinkers known as the founder of cultural Zionism; Simon Dubnow (1860–1941), Jewish-born Russian historian, writer and activist; Sholem Yankev Abramovich (Mendele Moher Sforim (1836–1917), Jewish author and one of the founders of modern Yiddish and Hebrew literature; Mosheh Leib Lilienblum (1843–1910), Jewish scholar and author; Yehudah Leib (Leon) Pinsker (1821–1891), physician, Zionist pioneer and activist, and the founder and leader of the *Hovevei Zion* (lovers of Zion) movement; Simon Frug, (1860–1916), multi-lingual Russian poet, lyricist and author; Yehoshua Rawnitzki (1859–1944), Hebrew publisher, editor, and collaborator of Bialik; Elhanan Lewinsky (1857–1910), Hebrew writer and Zionist leader; Hayim Nahman Bialik (1873–1934), Jewish poet who wrote primarily in Hebrew but also in Yiddish. Bialik was one of the pioneers of modern Hebrew poetry. He was part of the vanguard of Jewish thinkers who gave voice to the breath of new life in Jewish life.

[2] Avigdor Hameiri, *Bialik al Atar* (Tel Aviv: Niv, 1962), 14.

[3] Dan Meron, "Al Hahmei Odessa," In *Zman Yehudi Hadash, Tarbut Yehudit Be'eden Hiloni*, volume 3, Keter Publishing Company, Pozen Library and Association for Modern Hebrew Culture (Jerusalem: Spinoza Institute, 2007), 313.

[4] Meir Maidanik, "Be'ir Haharega," In *Reshumot – Me'asef Ledivrei Zihronot, Le'etnografia Ulefolklor Beyisrael,* first edition (Berlin: G. Druyanov, Moriah, 1923).

[5] Alexei Maximovich Peshkov, primarily known as Maxim Gorky (1868–1936), Russian and Soviet writer, a founder of the socialist realism literary method, and political activist.

[6] Avigdor Hameiri, "Habaita," *Hatekufa* (Berlin: Taz, Tammuz-Elul 1922), 307.

[7] Hameiri was very fond of movies and was the first film critic in the land of Israel as well as first acknowledged screenwriter of the first talking picture in Israel, *Zot Hi Haaretz.*

[8] Avigdor Hameiri, *Ben Laila Lelaila* (Tel Aviv: Yavneh, 1944), 207.

[9]Anton Ivanovich Denikin (1872–1947), White Army general during the Russian civil war, latterly active in Ukraine.

[10]Avigdor Feuerstein, "Mihtav laavadim velishefahot," *Lev Hadash*, 2, Yom Kippur eve 1927. Tel Aviv: 5.

[11]Avigdor Feuerstein, "Odessa – Silent Movie" (1920–1921), *Kav, Haaretz*, Wednesday 08.02.1922, volume 3.

[12]Avigdor Hameiri, *Hohmat Habehemoth* (Tel Aviv: 'Haaretz,' Press, 1933), 12–13.

[13]Vladimir Ilyich Ulyanov (1870–1924), Russian revolutionary, politician, and political theorist who served as head of government of Soviet Russia from 1917 to 1924 and of the Soviet Union from 1922 to 1924.

[14]Yehudah Leib (Leon) Gordon (1830–1892), among the most important Hebrew poets of the Jewish Enlightenment. Hameiri greatly admired Gordon; he was one of the only Hebrew poets he had known from his grandfather. In his second war novel *Bagehinom Shel Mata*, Hameiri described his experiences as a Russian prisoner of war (Avigdor Hameiri, *Hell on Earth*, translated and edited by Peter C. Appelbaum (Detroit: Wayne State University Press, 2017).

[15]Avigdor Hameiri, "Biyedei Adam," *Haaretz*, 12.03. 1926, 5.

[16]Avigdor Feuerstein, "Odessa — Silent Movie" (1920–1921), 2, *Le'am*, 24.08.1921, 2.

[17]Avigdor Hameiri, *Hayishuv* 26–27, 13 Nisan. 1925, 16–18.

[18]Idem., *Hayishuv* 29 Nisan 1925, 10–11.

[19]Idem., *Hayishuv* 4 Sivan 1925, 11–12.

[20]Kushta, Kosta: Istanbul (Ottoman Judaeo-Spanish)

[21]This piece does not appear in the 1929 edition, but in A. Hameiri, *Mivchar Sipurei Avigdor Hameiri* (Tel-Aviv: Hotza'at Idit. 1954): It is also reproduced in http://benyehuda.org/hameiri/bein_shiney_haadam.html.

[22]A parasitic infection that blocks lymph vessels, causing organs and limbs to swell and hypertrophy, sometimes grotesquely.

[23]Lev Davidovich Bronstein (Trotsky) (1879–1940), Soviet politician and founder of the Red Army.

[24]*Hashigaon hagadol,* Hameiri's first book on his service during the First World War Austro-Hungarian Army, 1914–1918. *The Great Madness,* translated by Yael Lotan (Haifa: Or Ron, 1984).

[25]Job 19:26. *Mibesari:* One of the most difficult verses in the entire book. Could also mean "without my flesh." Some expressions in Job only occur once, making it impossible to define their true meaning.

[26]*Hilula* is the anniversary of the death of a great *Tzaddik* (Hasidic righteous man), to be celebrated by joy and celebration, not mourning.

[27]*Anim Zemirot* (let us sing sweet songs): a Jewish liturgical poem (also known as *Shir Hakavod*) sung at the end of Sabbath and holiday morning services.

[28]*Areshet Sefateinu* (may the entreaty of our lips): prayer recited after blowing the shofar during the additional service of Rosh Hashanah morning (repeated three times).

[29]Jewish ritual slaughterer.

[30]The original says *biur chametz,* removal of all leaven just before Passover.

[31]A riff on 2 Samuel, 22: 26–27, and Psalm 18:26–27.

[32]Obadiah, 4. The verse ends — "thence I will bring you down, says the Lord."

[33]Solomon ibn Gabirol (ca. 1021–1022 to 1050–1070. Also known as Avicebron. Andalusian poet and Jewish philosopher.

[34]Hameiri is being sarcastic. The original says *areshet sefataim* (see note 28).

[35]Psalm 29:7.

[36]The Cheka (*chrezvychaynaya komissiya,* Emergency Committee), the first secret service of the nascent Soviet State, was created by Lenin, and led by Felix Dzerzhinsky (1877–1926). It subsequently morphed into the NKVD, and then the KGB.

[37]In Russian (unlike some other Slavic languages), *zhid* is a derogatory epithet. The polite form is *yevrey.*

[38]"Young Zionist" movement, founded in Russia in 1902.

[39]*Yeshivah* also means meeting, or gathering.

[40]Rabbi Yochanan said in the name of Rabbi Shimon ben Yehotzadak: "By a majority vote, it was resolved in the attic of Nitzah's house in Lod that, in every (other) law in the Torah, if a man is threatened 'transgress and not suffer death,' he may transgress and not suffer death — except for idolatry, incest (including sexual licentiousness) and murder (Sanhedrin 74a)."

[41]Hameiri was taken captive in June 1916 at the start of the Brusilov Offensive. For the story of his imprisonment, see A. Hameiri, *Hell on Earth* (see note 14).

[42]The first two lines of *Hatikvah* (The Hope), Israeli national anthem.

[43]Sotzobes: Department of the Social Relief of the Population. Soviet-style organization that provided help to various strata of the population such as war veterans, blind, mute, deaf, homeless, handicapped, etc.

[44]Used in the Russian sense of education, class, or breeding.

[45]Genesis 18, 27.

[46]Fonye the ganev: Derogatory Yiddish name for Nicholas II.

[47]Lamentations 5:8. The sentence ends: — "and there is no one to free us from their hands." The book of Lamentations is recited on *Tisha Be'av* (the Ninth of Av), the Jewish day of national mourning.

[48]Father.

[49]Jeremiah 10:25. These verses are recited during the second part of the Pesach seder when the door is symbolically opened to let the Prophet Elijah in. It is the one time in the year when Jews can ritually curse (in secret) those who have done them harm as a people.

[50]Sweet father.

[51]Hameiri sarcastically uses the word *hilula* a public celebration in memory of a saintly rabbi.

[52]Talmud Yerushalmi Berachot 7b.

[53]Daniel 5:6.

[54]Recognized Hebrew/Yiddish word for cheek, or audacity.

[55]Proverbs 9:17. "Stolen water is sweet, and food eaten in secret is delicious."

[56]Joseph Fourier (1768–1830), French mathematician and physicist.

[57]*Nega'im* (blemishes), one of the tractates of the Mishnah (oral law) deals with leprosy and other boils or blemishes which might render ritual uncleanness. It also deals with "leprosy of houses," which must have been mold, mildew or insect invasions.

[58]Southern suburb of Odessa (between Odessa and Chornomorsk).

[59]A young *yeshivah* student.

[60]Untranslatable pun between *kina* (lamentation) and *kin'a* (envy).

[61]Sexton.

[62]An untranslatable pun between *mashkit* and *mashtik*.

[63]An ironic phrase, based on a Talmudic blessing a man says before going into a privy, to prevent his guardian angels from joining him there (Berachot 60b).

[64]Non-Jew. Sometimes used perjoratively.

[65]Gittin 40b.

[66]The original *sar ha'elef* (captain of a thousand) has no exact modern equivalent.

[67]Hameiri sarcastically uses "Be Honored," the beginning of the prayer for the toilet described above.

[68]The Volga Germans (Volga Deutsche) were invited by Catherine the Great into Russia, to farm Russian lands while maintaining their language and culture. Jews were nor permitted entry.

[69]Original: "Their etrog became damaged." An etrog is a citron used on the festival of tabernacles (Sukkoth).

[70]Regimental commander.

[71]*Epikores.* A Hebrew word of Greek origin cited in the Mishnah, referring literally to one who does not have a share in the world to come:

[72]The *Haskalah*, or Jewish Enlightenment, was an intellectual movement in Europe that lasted from approximately the 1770s to the 1880s. The *Haskalah* was inspired by the European Enlightenment but had a Jewish character.

[73]Peretz Smolenskin (1842–1885), Russian Hebrew novelist and editor, a leading figure of late Hebrew Haskalah and a precursor of Zionism; Avraham Mapu (1808–1867), Lithuanian Hebrew novelist of the *Haskalah,*

author of the first Hebrew novel, *Love of Zion* (1853). The Josippon is a medieval chronicle of Jewish history from Adam to the age of Titus believed to have been written by Josippon or Joseph ben Gorion (Pseudo-Josephus). "The book of the Apple" is a short philosophical text, composed in Arabic probably in the 10th century and translated to Hebrew in 1235, traditionally (yet wrongly) ascribed to Aristotle (384–322 BCE); "The Dessauer" [Native of Dessau] and "Rambman" [acronym of Rabbi Moshe Ben Menachem] are both nicknames of Moses Mendelssohn (1729–1786), leading German-Jewish philosopher and founding father of Jewish Haskalah.

[74] A movement of Marxist–Zionist Jewish workers founded in various cities of Poland, Europe and the Russian Empire in about the turn of the twentieth century.

[75] Sanhedrin 111a.

[76] Proverbs 2:19.

[77] Genesis 15:14.

[78] "They beat me, they bruised me; they took away my cloak, those watchmen of the walls!" (Song of Songs 5:7).

[79] "Wounds and welts and open sores, not cleansed or bandaged or soothed with olive oil" (Isaiah 1:6).

[80] Isaiah 53:7.

[81] An untranslatable pun on the word *bei'ur,* (exegesis) and *bi'ur* (destruction).

[82] Moses de León (c. 1240–1305), also known as Moshe ben Shem-Tov, Spanish rabbi and Kabbalist considered the composer or redactor of the Zohar (book of Jewish mysticism). It is a matter of controversy if the Zohar is his own work, or if he committed traditions going back to Rabbi Shimon bar Yochai, a second century sage.

[83] Micha Josef Berdyczewski (1865–1921), Ukrainian-born Hebrew writer, journalist and scholar; Isaac Leib Peretz (1852–1915), Polish-born Yiddish author and playwright.

[84] *Hilula.*

[85] Shimon bar Yochai (see note 82) was a 2nd-century sage in ancient Israel, said to be active after the destruction of the Second Temple in 70 CE. He

was one of the most eminent disciples of Rabbi Akiva, and is pseudepigraphically attributed with the authorship of the Zohar, the chief work of Kabbalah.

[86]Short-lived Hungarian Soviet Republic, led by Béla Kun.

[87]Prayer recited to celebrate special occasions: "Blessed are You, Lord, our God, King of the Universe, who has granted us life, sustained us, and enabled us to reach this occasion."

[88]Because of the seventeenth century massacres of Jews, Jesuits, Uniates, and Polish nobility, the Polish language term *Hajdamactwo* became a pejorative label for Ukrainians as a whole.

[89]*Almaz* was a second-class cruiser in the Imperial Russian Navy. It was the only major ship to reach Vladivostok after the Battle of Tsushima (May 27–28, 1905). However, the crew revolted in early 1918 against the authority of the Ukrainian People's Republic, supporting the Odessa Soviet Republic. The ship became the center of a "peoples marine military tribunal," where many officers of the former Imperial Russian Navy were imprisoned, tortured and executed. In September 1918, while docked as Sevastopol, *Almaz* was captured by the White movement forces. In 1920 she was interned with the remainder of the White fleet.

[90]*Ekh, yablochko,* ("Ekh, little apple") also numerous versions: "Ekh little apple, where are you rolling?", "Ekh little apple on the saucer," etc., depending on the subsequent rhyme. A great number of verses of this kind proliferated during the Russian Civil War, both in Red and White camps. The song itself has nothing to do with apples, with its verse commonly being related to the political issues of the time.

[91]"They traded with you in choice garments, in clothes of blue and embroidered work, and in carpets of many colors and tightly wound cords, which were among your merchandise. The ships of Tarshish were the carriers for your merchandise. And you were filled and were very glorious in the heart of the seas." Ezekiel 27: 24–25.

[92]"Shattered by the sea in the depths of the waters; your wares and all your company have gone down with you." Ezekiel 27:34.

[93]According to history books, it was named before the war.

[94]An untranslatable pun between *lifrot* (to cash in) and *limrot* (to pluck).

[95]Baruch (Benedict) Spinoza (1632–1677), Dutch philosopher of Sephardi/Jewish origin who laid the groundwork for eighteenth-century enlightenment. According to Spinoza, the highest virtue is the intellectual love or knowledge of God/Nature/Universe. Spinoza was excommunicated from his Amsterdam synagogue for daring to postulate unity of God and nature. Logos: the word of God.

[96]Vengerskiy.

[97]The Cheka (All-Russian Emergency Commission for Combating Counter-Revolution and Sabotage) was created on December 20, 1917, after a decree issued by Lenin.

[98]Fyodor Mikhailovich Dostoyevsky (1821–1881), Russian novelist, short story writer, essayist, journalist and philosopher.

[99]Unfinished opera by Sergei Rachmaninov (1873–1943).

[100]"To life." Hebrew toast.

[101]Nestor Ivanovich Makhno (1888–1934), Ukrainian anarcho-communist.

[102]Mishka Japonchik (lit. "Mikey the Jap") (1891–1919), Odessa gangster, Jewish revolutionary and Soviet military leader.

[103]After Juvenal (late first and early second century CE): *difficile est saturam non scribere* (it is difficult not to write satire).

[104]Leaven (forbidden on Pesach).

[105]Sanhedrin 81b.

[106]Yuriy (Yurko) Yosipovich Tyutyunnyk (1891–1930), Ukrainian nationalist general.

[107]*Biur chametz* — removal of all leaven before Pesach.

[108]The *Keren Kayemet LeYisrael* was founded in 1901, to buy and develop land in Ottoman Palestine (later British Mandate for Palestine, and subsequently Israel and the Palestinian territories) for Jewish settlement.

[109]Indeed, Modern Hebrew is singularly lacking in obscenities, having been derived from the Bible by Eliezer Ben Yehudah (1858–1922).

[110]Chudak.

[111]Anatoly Vasilyevich Lunacharsky (1875–1933), Russian Marxist revolutionary.

[112]Latvian Red riflemen played an important part in the Russian Revolution 1917–1922; many Cheka officers were Latvian. Yakov Peters (1886–1938) was Deputy Chairman of the Cheka from 1918 and briefly the acting Chairman of the Cheka from 7 July to 22 August 1918.

[113]Tsar Nicholas, his wife and five children were murdered in Yekaterinberg on 17 July, 1918.

[114]Yakov Mikhailovich Yurovsky (1878–1938) was the chief executioner of the Tsar and his family.

[115]Mosheh Kleinman (1871–1948), Hebrew and Yiddish publisher and newspaper editor.

[116]Described in the last chapter of *Hell on Earth*.

[117]Alter Druyanov (1870–1938), author, folklorist, and Zionist public official.

[118]Ginda Abramovna from Kiev, whom Hameiri later marries (first described in *Hell on Earth*).

About the Author

Avigdor Hameiri (Feuerstein, 1890–1970) was a Hebrew poet (the first Poet Laureate of Israel), novelist, editor, and translator. Hameiri was born in Dávidháza, Carpatho-Ruthenia (then Hungary but present-day Ukraine). His first Hebrew poem "Ben he-Atid," appeared in the weekly *Ha-Mizpeh* (1907). His first volume of verse, entitled *Mi-Shirei Avigdor Feuerstein,* was published  in 1912. In 1916 he was captured by the Russians while serving as an Austrian officer on the Russian front, imprisoned in Siberia, and released in 1917 after the October Revolution. In 1921 he immigrated to Palestine, joined the staff of the daily *Haaretz,* and edited several journals. In Tel Aviv, he founded the first Hebrew social satirical theater, *Ha-Kumkum* (1932). Hameiri published a number of novels, short stories, and poetry collections that gave literary expression to his war experiences, the Third Aliyah, and later, the Holocaust. In his work he attacked the stagnation of Jewish life, described the carnage and hatred that engulfed all of humanity during World War I and particularly the vulnerability of Jews of this time to its consequences. Hameiri's power as a storyteller is most revealed in his war stories; observational, often cinematic in the vividness of the moment and place capturing the peculiarly tragic fate of the Jewish soldier fighting wars which are not his, and of the Jewish residents' fate in wars' aftermath. He won the Bialik Prize in 1936 and the Israel Prize in 1938 and again in 1968. His other works of fiction include the important novel *Ha-Shiga'on ha-Gadol* (*The Great Madness*—a new translation forthcoming 2021). His books have been published in 12 languages. He died in Israel on April 3, 1970.

About the Editor/Translator

Peter C. Appelbaum, MD, PhD, is Emeritus Professor of Pathology, Pennsylvania State University College of Medicine. After more than four decades in infectious disease research, Dr. Appelbaum is spending his retirement years writing and translating books on modern-day Jewish military history. He is the author of *Loyalty Betrayed: Jewish Chaplains in the German Army during the First World War* and *Loyal Son: Jews in the German Army in the Great Wars* (Vallentine-Mitchell, 2014) and, together with James Scott, has translated an anthology of war essays and poems by Kurt Tucholsky (*Prayer after the Slaughter*, Berlinica, 2015) and *Broken Carousel: German Jewish Soldier-Poets of the Great War* (Stone Tower Books, 2017). He is also the translator/editor of *Jewish Tales of the Great War* (Stone Tower Books, 2017). Dr. Appelbaum has also translated *Hell on Earth* by Avigdor Hameiri into English from the original Hebrew for the first time (Wayne State University Press, fall, 2017). For that work, he was the recipient of the TLS-Risa Domb/Porjes Prize for Hebrew-English Translation for 2019. He is also the translator and editor of *Carnage and Care on the Eastern Front: The War Diaries of Bernhard Bardach, 1914–1918* (Berghahn Books, 2018).

The Sea and Other Poems by Guillevic.
Translated by Patricia Terry. Introduction
by Monique Chefdor.

Through Naked Branches by Tarjei Vesaas.
Translated, edited, and introduced by
Roger Greenwald.

To Speak, to Tell You? Poems by Sabine Sicaud.
Translated by Norman R. Shapiro. Introduction
and notes by Odile Ayral-Clause.

MODERN POETRY SERIES

BARNSTONE, WILLIS.
ABC of Translation
African Bestiary (forthcoming)

BRINKS, DAVE.
The Caveat Onus
The Secret Brain: Selected Poems 1995–2012

CESEREANU, RUXANDRA.
Crusader-Woman. Translated by Adam J.
    Sorkin. Introduction by Andrei Codrescu.
Forgiven Submarine by Ruxandra Cesereanu
    and Andrei Codrescu.

ESHLEMAN, CLAYTON.
An Alchemist with One Eye on Fire
Anticline
Archaic Design
Clayton Eshleman/The Essential Poetry: 1960–2015
Grindstone of Rapport: A Clayton Eshleman Reader
Penetralia
Pollen Aria
The Price of Experience
Endure: Poems by Bei Dao. Translated by
    Clayton Eshleman and Lucas Klein.
Curdled Skulls: Poems of Bernard Bador. Translated
    by Bernard Bador with Clayton Eshleman.

JORIS, PIERRE.
Barzakh (Poems 2000–2012)
Exile Is My Trade: A Habib Tengour Reader

KALLET, MARILYN.
How Our Bodies Learned
The Love That Moves Me
Packing Light: New and Selected Poems
Disenchanted City (La ville désenchantée)
    by Chantal Bizzini. Translated by J.
    Bradford Anderson, Darren Jackson, and
    Marilyn Kallet.

KELLY, ROBERT.
Fire Exit
The Hexagon

KESSLER, STEPHEN.
Garage Elegies

LAVENDER, BILL.
Memory Wing

LEVINSON, HELLER.
from stone this running
LinguaQuake
Seep
Tenebraed
Un-
Wrack Lariat

OLSON, JOHN.
Backscatter: New and Selected Poems
Dada Budapest
Larynx Galaxy
Weave of the Dream King (forthcoming)

OSUNDARE, NIYI.
City Without People: The Katrina Poems

ROBERTSON, MEBANE.
An American Unconscious
Signal from Draco: New and Selected Poems

ROTHENBERG, JEROME.
Concealments and Caprichos
Eye of Witness: A Jerome Rothenberg Reader.
    Edited with commentaries by Heriberto
    Yepez & Jerome Rothenberg.
The President of Desolation & Other Poems

SAÏD, AMINA.
The Present Tense of the World: Poems 2000–2009.
    Translated with an introduction by
    Marilyn Hacker.

SHIVANI, ANIS.
Soraya (Sonnets)

WARD, JERRY W., JR.
Fractal Song

ANTHOLOGIES / BIOGRAPHIES

*Barbaric Vast & Wild: A Gathering of Outside and
Subterranean Poetry (Poems for the Millennium,*
vol. 5). Editors: Jerome Rothenberg and
John Bloomberg-Rissman

Clayton Eshleman: The Whole Art
by Stuart Kendall

Revolution of the Mind: The Life of André Breton
by Mark Polizzotti

WWW.BLACKWIDOWPRESS.COM

ALSO AVAILABLE FROM STONE TOWER PRESS

Giving voice to the experiences of war is something that frequently is expressed best through the words of poets who can speak with one voice for many soldiers. Their words convey emotions, sentiments, and experiences that are often too difficult for others to express. There are many familiar names among the war poets of the First World War, but most of them are British. What largely is absent and overlooked is the perspective of soldiers from the Central Powers. This volume provides English and German readers the poetry of German Jewish soldiers. Among the many poets presented are: Immanuel Saul, Samuel Jacobs, Leo Sternberg, Ernst Toller, and Kurt Tucholsky. Breathtaking and heartbreaking, the poems show that the traumas of war know neither boundaries nor national allegiance.

The First World War changed the lives of millions of soldiers and civilians. Though many often think of the Western Front, there was also the oft-forgotten Eastern Front from which the writings in this book are derived. Selig Schachnowitz, a gentle soul who wrote much of his work in Yiddish, provides four short stories, each on a different topic about the war. Dr. Felix Theilhaber—a decorated physician in the German Army—laconically describes his meeting and experiences with the shtetl Jews of Eastern Europe—their language, foibles, view of war, and religious practices. These writings provide creative glimpses of the war that are often overlooked. They remind readers of the tragedy of war on an intensely personal level.

stonetowerpress.com